The Teutonic Knights

by
John Wharem

authorHOUSE®

AuthorHouse™
1663 Liberty Drive, Suite 200
Bloomington, IN 47403
www.authorhouse.com
Phone: 1-800-839-8640

©*2008 John Wharem. All rights reserved.*

No part of this book may be reproduced, stored in a retrieval system, or transmitted by any means without the written permission of the author.

First published by AuthorHouse   2/25/2008

ISBN: 978-1-4343-7013-6 (e)
ISBN: 978-1-4343-7012-9 (sc)

Library of Congress Control Number: 2008901667

Printed in the United States of America
Bloomington, Indiana

This book is printed on acid-free paper.

Disclaimer

This book is a science fiction story. Although some biblical references have been used, this book is not to be taken literally.

Table of Contents

Introduction 1

Chapter 1: The Cong Threat 7

Chapter 2: The Evacuation 27

Chapter 3: Fighter Training 43

Chapter 4: Pirate Transfers 55

Chapter 5: The Highlander Station 71

Chapter 6: An Important Assignment 97

Chapter 7: Trynocn 7 117

Chapter 8: A Trip to Brotherhood 137

Chapter 9: Return to the Panther 153

Chapter 10: Into the Labyrinth 167

Chapter 11: A New Assignment 185

Introduction

The year is 2010 A.D.; an archeologist named Joash has just discovered the remains of an ancient city. He enters the largest building in the city. There he discovers a number of books. He pulls one from a shelf and opens it. The writing is in a language that he has never seen before. He puts the book back. He hears a voice say, "Akabdule nintoe ke-at brookas."

Joash is surprised and a little afraid, and he asks, "Is anyone here?"

The voice replies, "Questing facts hoard. Gratify persist vernacular." Joash noticed that this time, the voice spoke in English. The words didn't make much sense, but the last two could mean that the voice wanted him to continue talking.

Joash asks, "Who are you?"

The voice says, "I believe that I have identified your language. I am Library Artificial Computing Intelligence 0592. You can call me L.A.C.I. or Laci if you wish."

Joash replies, "So you are an automated librarian, and this building was the town's library?"

Laci responds, "That is correct, sir. May I assist you with an inquiry?"

Joash quietly says, "Amazing. This city must be at least 3,000 years old, and it has an interactive computer." Then he replies to Laci, "Yes, I would like to know about the civilization who built this city."

Laci answers, "Of course, follow the red arrows on the floor. They will lead you to the history section." Joash looks down and sees a series of red arrows appearing on the floor. He follows them to a bookcase in the center of the room. He takes out a book and notices that it has the same strange writing as the first book he opened.

Joash says, "I can't read this language. Could you help me translate it?"

Laci replies, "Oh, my apologies. Since you don't speak our language, I should have guessed that you wouldn't be able to read it. Please replace the book." After Joash puts the book back on the shelf, he sees a blue light run across the top of all the books.

Laci says, "You should be able to read them now."

Joash pulls the book out, and he notices that he can now read the cover. It reads <u>The Teutonic Knights: Christian's Quest</u>.

Joash asks, "How did you do that?"

Laci responds, "Given your country's current level of technology, I don't believe that you would understand."

Joash asks, "How do you know my country's level of technology?"

Laci answers, "This city was built to monitor the development of the nations that still occupy this world. Although you are the first organic in this city in quite a long time, the city's computers continue to monitor the outside world. As a Library Artificial Computing Intelligence, I am privy to any information compiled by the city's other computers. Your language identified the country where you were born, or at least where you were raised."

Joash asks, "Why was this city built to monitor our nation's development, and what happened to the people who built it?"

Laci replies, "The ones who built this city left it hundreds of years ago. Their departure had something to do with them wanting to interact with the outside world, instead of simply observing it. Organics can be so irrational at times. As for the reason this city was built, if you read the history books before you, I am sure you will find your answer. You may also find the answers to many other questions that I'm sure you have. However, I do recommend that you start at the beginning."

Joash asks, "Where is that?" One of the books begins to glow and Joash tries to pull it out, but it won't budge.

Laci says, "Please replace the book that you have now, before you take out another. We must keep the library neat and tidy after all."

Joash puts the book, *Christian's Quest* back on the shelf and is then able to pull out the glowing book. Joash begins to read the book, and the following is what he read.

In 2159 B.C., there were three industrial civilizations on the Earth. The first civilization was the Congs. The Congs were a deceptive people whose only concern was the accumulation of worldly treasures. They were just about to enter the atomic age when this story takes place.

The second civilization was the Highlanders. The Highlanders were a warrior people who had a great deal of civil liberties, arguably the most important of these being the freedom of religion. They had been traveling through space for about one-hundred years, when this story takes place.

The third civilization was the Teutonics. The Teutonics were a God-fearing people, and had been since one of the shepherd kings told them about the one true God—Jehovah. The Teutonics quickly accepted this belief and began to worship only Jehovah. Since that day, the Teutonics were blessed with prosperity and scientific achievement. They had begun colonizing space over 200 years before this story takes place.

This story centers on the Teutonics' departure from Earth and their new home among the stars. Before I can tell you the story, you must understand that the Teutonic political system at that time was based on the belief that it was better to do nothing than to do the wrong thing. Their political power was divided between the various members of the House of Representatives. The King has 12 percent of the political power. He represents the tradition and customs of older days and is a reminder of the rules and regulations that were written in the protected laws when the Teutonic tribes first united into a nation. The Arch Duke has 8 percent of the political power. He represents the combat side of the Teutonics and the need every great civilization has for exploration and change. Both the King and Arch Duke are hereditary titles, passed from parent to child; however the differences that they each represent has made the kings and arch dukes long time political rivals. The leader of the Teutonic Knights, called the Teutonic Leader, has 10 percent of the political power. He represents the Teutonic's close connection to The Lord God, as well as the great contribution that the Teutonic Knights made as spiritual guides and protectors of the rest of the Teutonic citizens. The Teutonic Knights themselves select who will serve as their leader. Once appointed, the Teutonic Leader retains his or her position until he chooses to retire, dies or is impeached. In the time before this book takes place, no Teutonic Leader had ever been impeached, but being a cautious people, the ability to do so was written into the Protected Laws long ago. The remaining 70 percent of the political power is divided among the elected representatives who represent the common people. Every Teutonic citizen, great or small, has the right to vote for whomever they want the representatives of their tribes to be. The tribes had different ways of determining who could run for office and how long they could hold that office. The representatives would typically serve a five-year term, and then they would run for reelection. A few tribes also limited the number of terms each representative could have. In order to make a governing decision, at least 65 percent of the political power, or 70 percent of the Teutonic people needed to agree. To pass a new law, at least 70 percent of the political power, or 80 percent of the Teutonic people needed to sign the bill . In order to amend the protected laws, either at least 87 percent of the political power, or at least 90 percent of the Teutonic people needed to sign the bill.

The Teutonic Knights was an organization dedicated to protecting the Teutonic citizens from both internal and external threats. The Teutonic Knights were similar to the prophets of Israel, in that they had a very close connection to God. God talked to them both through the Spirit and through messengers. God also protected them from harm and gave them powers similar to what He gave Moses, Elijah, and the other prophets. However, this closeness to God was dependent upon the level of the Knight's faith; for if they did not believe in something, they could not claim it.

Chapter 1: The Cong Threat

Today, the Arch Duke has called a conference with the rest of the House of Representatives. The reason for this conference is to discuss the increasing threat of a major Cong attack and to determine how the Teutonic civilization should respond.

The King starts the meeting by saying, "First of all, let me remind everyone here that the Congs do not even have the atomic bomb yet. In my opinion, any attack they made on us would be suicidal."

The Arch Duke replies, "Just because the Congs have yet to split the atom does not mean that they are not dangerous."

The Duke holds up a piece of paper, points at it and continues, "This report tells us that the Congs have developed a hypnotic ray that makes men and woman believe whatever the Congs tell them. The Congs have been using this ray to convince the citizens of Earth that every Teutonic is evil and must be destroyed."

The King responds, "I find that hard to believe. From what source did you get this report?"

The Arch Duke uses his hand to call forward a Teutonic Knight, who had been patently waiting at the back of the room. Then the Arch Duke answers, "David has been gathering intelligence on the Congs' new weapon for the last six months. If you don't believe me, ask him yourself. You all know that Teutonic Knights are forbidden to lie."

The King turns to David and asks, "How is it possible that you could have been gathering intelligence for six months without the Congs noticing? Is it not possible that they discovered you were spying on them and falsified their reports in order to make us think that they were more advanced than they really are?"

David replies, "I'm part of the reconnaissance division. I've been trained in infiltration and intelligence gathering, and this includes training in the art of invisibility. Every morning I prayed that God would hide me under the shadow of his wings, and the Lord answered my prayer. He hid me from the Cong's view. Since they could not see me, I did not have to read reports. Instead, I walked right into their weapon testing area and saw firsthand the effect this ray had on people."

Then the King asked, "Is this weapon as powerful as the arch duke tells us? Can it control the minds of men and women?"

David answers, "Yes, sir. It can."

The King sits down in his chair and solemnly says, "If this ray is so powerful, how can we hope to defeat the Congs?"

David interrupts and responds, "Sir," but he catches himself and remembers that, since he is not a representative, he does not have the right to address the House unless he is asked a question.

The King turns to David and replies, "What? If you have something relevant to say, do not hesitate to speak."

David continues, "The ray dose not work on Teutonic Knights for God protects us from deception. In fact, the ray doesn't work on anyone who has a close connection to the Lord God. Also, the Highlanders have developed a counter field which blocks the ray's effects in localized areas."

The King stands up and facing the Arch Duke asks, "What do you propose we do?"

The Arch Duke responds, "We should attack the Congs and destroy their hypnotic rays and research facilities. We should also begin preparations for "Project Evacuation."

The King says, "Project Evacuation is only to be used in an extreme emergency."

The Arch Duke responds, "Don't you think that having almost everyone on the planet trying to kill us is an extreme emergency?"

The King asks, "But if you destroy the hypnotic rays and the technology behind them, won't that solve the problem?"

The Arch Duke answers, "Destroying the hypnotic rays and the technology behind them will stop the Congs from using the rays again, but it won't erase the lies that are already in the people's heads."

The King replies, "Isn't there any other way? Do we really need to leave our home?"

The Arch Duke responds, "I'm sorry. I love this planet as much as you do, but the only way we could stay would be to kill all the people who the Congs have used the ray on. That is something that we as followers of Jehovah cannot do. It would go against God's will. We are to harm no one, if there is a way to peacefully coexist with them."

The King says, "We have heard the situation and are presented with the options. May God help us to make the right choice."

The rest of the people in the House said, "Amen." David leaves the room as the representatives begin to cast their votes.

After the meeting is adjourned, David asks the Arch Duke, "What did the House decide?"

The Arch Duke answers David, "The House decided to take both of my suggestions. Even the King, despite his dislike of me, has voted in favor of my proposal."

David says, "That must be a first."

The Arch Duke responds, "It is a rare thing for the king to agree with me, but in this case, he must have realized that change was needed."

David asks, "What did the king mean by 'leave our home?' What is Project Evacuation?"

The Arch Duke answers, "As you know, for the past 200 years, we have been sending colony ships to habitable planets in the 'Star Galaxy'. We have also been planning to join any willing planets together into one Teutonic Union."

David nods and says, "Yes, but what does that have to do with us all leaving Earth?"

The Arch Duke replies, "When the House began to recognize the possibility that the Congs could eventually become a threat, they created Project Evacuation. They used the cosmic telescopes to search the Star Galaxy and found the largest unpopulated, habitable planet, which the House named Brotherhood. Next, the House put that planet's coordinates into the inverted gateways. They also built a massive ship called the Hopeful to carry the inverted gateways and the rest of our buildings to Brotherhood.

David says, "I see, so Project Evacuation is a plan to relocate our civilization to Brotherhood. What about the Messiah? How will we know when He arrives, if we are in another galaxy?"

The Arch Duke answers, "We will leave a small number of remnant cities on earth. Their mission will be to remain hidden and secretly monitor the other nations. They will await the coming of the Messiah. Once He comes, the remnant will transmit the news and all of His teachings to us. Once the Messiah is born, we can probably even return home."

David replies, "It is a good plan, but I am sorry that we will have to use it."

The Arch Duke says, "So am I."

After David and the Arch Duke are through with their discussion, David goes to his room in the Knight's Palace and changes out of his dress uniform. After changing into everyday clothing, he goes into the central living space that is attached to his room. Off of this room are three other rooms just like his. David thinks about each of his friends who occupy the other rooms. He thinks first of the friend named Adino, who occupies the first room on the left. David remembers how Adino is always ready for a fight and how often John, who is the youngest of the four, by two years, always has to hold Adino back whenever these warrior tendencies take hold of him. Lastly, David thinks of

Joshua, who has been his best friend since they were five years old and occupies the room directly opposite his own.

It has been six months since David has seen any of them and he's looking forward to spending time with his friends. As he knocks on each door, he receives no response.

"They must all be out, probably on assignment. I guess I'll have to wait a little bit longer to see them," David thinks to himself.

In about an hour, John comes back. When John goes into the center room he sees David. John says, "Hey, David, when did you get back?"

David answers, "This morning, but I wasn't able to come back to the Knight's Palace until the House had made its decision. That was about an hour ago."

John asks David, "How did your mission go?"

David replies, "Well, I gathered enough intelligence to convince the House that we had to attack the Congs. I guess that means that I did a good job."

John says, "So then the House decided that our only option was to fight? It's too bad that there is no other way, but I'm sure that the House would not have made that decision unless it was absolutely necessary."

John and David hear a voice say, "So we're finally going to give the Congs what they deserve." John and David turn around to see Adino standing in the doorway.

John looks at Adino and responds, "It's a good thing that God doesn't give us what we deserve or none of us would be here."

Adino is about to reply, but David says, "Oh, come on, I just got back from a six-month mission. Can't you two wait until tomorrow to start arguing?"

John turns to David and says, "You're right. We should concentrate on happy things, not fighting. I won't talk about the Congs anymore today."

Adino responds, "Of course not, you got the last word, but this is David's homecoming." Adino lets out a small sigh and then continues, "I will not argue either."

David thinks, "That was the shortest fight those two ever had. Maybe I should go away more often."

David, Adino, and John all sat down and began to talk about what happened to them during the last six months.

David learns that John is being assigned as Elijah's Teutonic squire. Being paired with Elijah as an instructor is the one thing that half of the Teutonic squires pray for and the other half fear. Elijah is one of the most sought-after instructors, because he has more faith than all the other Teutonic Instructors and most of the Teutonic Teachers. This faith seems to rub off on his squires. Yet. he is one of the most dreaded instructors, because he is very strict and also has a habit of saying and doing things that seem to make no logical sense. What is even more frustrating is that when Elijah defies earthly logic, things always seem to work out for the best.

David also learns that Adino has been accepted into the Teutonic Royal Guard and begins special training next month. David is very pleased that the greatest warriors in the Teutonic Knights chose Adino as a member, but he wonders how Adino will handle the politics that come along with being assigned to guard the members of the Teutonic royal family.

David is also a little bit sad that his friends all seem to be moving in different directions. Just then Joshua walks into the room.

Joshua says, "David! When did you get back?"

David answers, "Quite awhile ago. I gave my report to the Arch Duke this morning and he brought me with him to address the House."

Joshua says, "That explains why I didn't see you in the pilot tryouts today."

David says, "The pilot tryouts were today? Shoot! I missed all the other tryouts because of my mission. Now I'm going to be stuck on reconnaissance for another year."

Josh says, "The tryouts aren't over yet. If you hurry, you can catch the last tryout session."

David quickly says thanks and then rushes to the simulator room. When David returns about an hour later, his friends ask him how he did.

David exclaims, "I must have done pretty well. I got assigned to Ace Squadron!"

Then Josh says, "So did I. Looks like we're going to be around each other awhile longer."

David feels glad that at least one of his friends is going to the same place he is.

The next morning the evacuation begins. While the main body of Teutonic Knights fight the Cong army, a small detachment of knights led by the Arch Duke and include David and Adino are sent to destroy the weapons testing area and the research facilities.

When the detachment arrives at the weapons testing area, the Teutonic Knights find patrols on every side.

Adino (who always focused his studies more on straight confrontation then stealth or faith combat) asks, "How are we going to get past those patrols without them activating the alarm?"

The Arch Duke replies, "David will lead us in a prayer that will hide us from their sight. Just repeat after him, and have faith."

David closes his eyes and begins to pray, "Almighty God, You are the Lord of the seen and the unseen. We humbly ask that you will make us unseen by our enemies. Please hide us under the shadow of your wings. Amen." The other Knights repeat after him, and soon they are all hidden from sight.

Once the Knights are in the research facility, they separate into two teams. Team Alpha (made up of only the Arch Duke, David and Adino) heads to the data storage room; while Team Beta (a much larger group consisting of the remaining Teutonic Knights) heads to the weapons testing area. Team Alpha's objective is to erase all the information within the computer system. Team Beta's objective is to destroy the Cong's hypnotic ray prototypes and any other new weapons that the Congs may have developed.

The research facility is built like a fortress. It's made out of super heated steel and equipped with a detection grid. It also has see-through power conduits running along the walls of the corridors. Because you are able to see the power flowing through these conduits, it is easy for repair people to quickly trace any break in the power flow. The fact that you can see the power flowing through these conduits also makes them appear quite beautiful, but they are deadly! If an enemy were to slam someone into one of them hard enough to break the transparent glass, the energy would fry his/her body until there was little more than ashes left.

When the members of Team Alpha reach the research storage section, they discover that there are a large number of Highlander sentry bots guarding the entrance to the data storage room. Team Alpha stays just out of the sentries' hearing range.

Adino asks, "Does this mean that the Highlanders are in league with the Congs? I thought they hated each other."

The arch duke answers, "No, the Congs must have zapped a few Highlander scientists before they were able to develop the counter field."

David says, "Well, what are we going to do? We can't just let the Congs keep these sentry bots. We can't destroy the bots, because as soon as we act aggressively, we will no longer be hidden and the detection grid will activate the alarm.

The arch duke turns to David and says, "In your report, didn't you say that there was a control hub for the detection grid?"

David answers, "Yes, but we can't destroy the hub because that would activate the backup alarm."

The Arch Duke says, "Can't we deactivate the backup alarm?"

David says, "The backup alarm and the hub are protected by level five barrier fields. As soon as we move against either one, we will become visible and the other will activate the alarm system."

Adino asks, "What if we destroy them both at the same time?"

David replies, "That could work. If we throw our laser disks at the same split second, they would pierce the barriers and destroy both targets before either had a chance to trigger the alarm system."

The Arch Duke says, "Well that sounds like our best bet."

Adino says, "Okay. Let's do this!"

The Arch Duke Asks David, "How do I get to the backup alarm?"

David says, "You go down that corridor until it intersects with another. Then you turn right. The backup alarm is at the end of the second corridor. Adino and I will head toward the hub."

The Arch Duke says, "We'll split up. Remember, don't destroy the hub until you call me on your wrist communicator so that we can synchronize our attacks."

David and Adino both respond, "Don't worry; we'll remember."

The Arch Duke says, "All right, let's go!," and they all head toward their objectives.

When Adino and David reach the field protecting the hub, David opens his wrist communicator and says, "David to Arch Duke; are you in position?"

The Arch Duke responds, "Yes, are you ready?" David tells Adino to get his laser disk ready. Then David tells the Arch Duke that they are ready. The Arch Duke says, "All right, on the count of three. One, two, three."

As the Arch Duke reaches three, they all throw their laser disks. The laser disks strike their targets at the same time! The knights are rewarded with a satisfying zzts sound as the hub and backup alarm are destroyed.

The Arch Duke tells David and Adino to meet him back at the entrance to the data storage room, and in no time the three are back together again.

Once the Arch Duke, David, and Adino are back together, the Arch Duke says, "David, get into the data storage room and wipe all the files from the hard drive. Adino and I will take care of these sentry bots." David, being closer to the bots and not wanting to be overheard, only nods in agreement.

As soon as the three knights become visible, Adino severs one of the bot's heads from its body. The Arch Duke slices diagonally with the tip of his blade cutting a bot from the shoulder to the waist as David moves toward the entrance of the data storage room.

Just as David is about to enter the storage room, one of the bots hits the switch to the entrance's blast door. Adino sees that the door will drop on David's head. David also sees it. In the blink of an eye, Adino lunges to push David out of the way, but at the same time David rolls forward. Adino flies over David, and slides into the data storage room. The blast door thuds shut and Adino is trapped.

David sees Adino locked behind the blast door, and David tells Adino, "You're going to have to purge the hard drive."

Adino says, "But I don't know how."

David says, "Don't worry, I'll talk you through the procedure. Open your wrist communicator and head towards to back part of the storage room."

Adino opens his wrist communicator. Just then the Arch Duke who's been trying to fight off the fifty or so bots yells, "I could use some help over here!" David rushes into the fray.

Adino reaches the back of the data storage room. He opens his wrist communicator and says, "I'm here. Now what?"

David says, "I can't help you unless I can see the hard drive."

Adino says, "Oh, sorry." He activates the monitor mode on his wrist communicator, and says, "Is that better?"

David thrusts his blade through one of the bots, and then answers, "Much better; the first step is to open the maintenance cover."

Adino says, "There's got to be over twenty covers! Which one do I open?"

David uses the broad side of his blade to block a few incoming shots and then says, "It's the one marked maintenance."

Adino exclaims, "None of them are marked maintenance! Don't you think that if one of them said maintenance, I would have already opened it, instead of asking you which one I should open? All that the covers have on them are funny little symbols."

David severs one of the bot's heads, and then says, "Sorry, I forgot that you can't read Cong, but there's no reason to get upset. The maintenance cover is the one with the symbol that looks like a bird and snake dancing."

Adino whispers, "I'm stuck in here, playing with computers, while he's out there having all the fun and he tells me that there's no reason to get upset." Adino says to David, "Okay, I've got the cover open. Now what?

David answers, "Turn the communicator towards the opening, so I can see inside." Adino does as he is told. Then he waits for David to tell him the next step.

David trolls his blade around his head, decapitating the bot that was trying to sneak up on him, and then says, "Okay, you need to divert the beam without severing it."

Adino asks, "How do I do that?"

David says, "Gently push the broad side of your blade though the laser beam."

Adino does this, and then says, "Okay, what's next?"

David throws his laser disk through the chest of one of the bots, and says, "Reverse the yellow and black wires. This should activate the command override."

Adino reverses the wires, and says, "Done, what now?"

David leaps five feet in the air, and cuts a bot in half as he comes down. David says, "Good, now all you have to do is delete all the partitions from the hard drive."

Adino asks, "Do what to the what?"

David answers, "Delete all the partitions from the hard drive. There can't be anything left on the hard drive."

Adino says, "This is ridiculous."

Instead of following David's direction, he thrusts his blade through the hard drive."

David says, "I guess that works, too. Now get back here. With the hard drive *taken care of* the power to the data storage room will be out, and the blast door will be on manual control. There's a handle at the top right of the door frame. Keep turning it to the left until the blast door is raised enough for you to squeeze out through the bottom of the opening."

Adino gets out of the data storage room and rushes back to join the other two knights. He gets there just in time to see the last blow. Adino exclaims, "The fight's over? I only got to destroy one bot!"

The Arch Duke turns to Adino and says, "Don't worry. There will be plenty to fight when we rejoin the main force."

As the three knights head back to regroup with Team Beta, they see that the power conduits are still carrying a substantial amount of power somewhere.

The Arch Duke stops, turns toward David, and says, "I thought that by destroying the hard drive we would have broken the circuit and stopped the flow of power completely."

David responds, "It should have, but maybe this conduit is on a different circuit."

The Arch Duke says, "If this is a different circuit, it must lead to something important. Otherwise, it would have been integrated with the others on the main circuit."

David asks the Arch Duke, "Do you think we should investigate?"

The Arch Duke says, "I think it might be a good idea. What do the two of you think?"

David answers, "I think we should look into it. It might lead us to something important."

Adino answers, "I, too, think we should investigate. It might lead us to more sentry bots."

The three knights head off to investigate the strange power flow, but what they find shocks them. They discover a hidden research lab containing a completed atomic bomb.

David turns to the Arch Duke and says, "I thought that the Congs were supposed to be years away from discovering the power of the atom."

The Arch Duke says, "Their atomic research probably got a boost from the captured Highlander scientists."

Then David says, "If that is an atom bomb, then we must move it out of here. The Congs can't be allowed to have atomic power at their disposal. It wouldn't matter to us, but all the undeveloped civilizations could easily be destroyed by atomic bombs."

Adino says, "Then we must destroy it and this research lab."

David says, "We can't destroy the bomb here! We're in the middle of one of the Congs' major cities. If we detonate it, the explosion would kill hundreds of thousands of people."

Adino responds, "Hundreds of thousands of Congs, you mean."

David says, "I mean hundreds of thousands of woman and children. Besides, we have no way of knowing how far the radiation will spread."

Adino says, "Well, then what should we do? We don't have enough people to move it."

Just then Team Beta arrives, and their leader says, "We've been looking all over for you guys. When you didn't show up at the exit, we began to think that you might need some help."

The Arch Duke says, "Well, you were right." The Arch Duke turns to David and Adino, and says, "See how the Lord provides? Now we have enough people to move the bomb."

The leader of Team Beta asks, "What bomb and where are we moving it to?"

The Arch Duke answers, "To answer the first part of your question, we are moving this atom bomb."

One of the other people in Team Beta, the only girl in this small group of knights asks the Arch Duke, "What about the second part of his question? Where are we going to move this bomb? None of us have enough faith to hide it from view. I think the Cong patrols would notice an atomic bomb floating out of the research facility."

David says, "We could use the emergency exit. I found it when I was gathering intelligence on the Congs. It starts with an underground tunnel, then goes through a cave, and the cave's exit is never heavily guarded."

The Arch Duke says, "That should work perfectly." Addressing the girl, he asks, "Do you have any demolition packs left?"

The girl responds, "We have three left." As she hands them to the Arch Duke, she asks, "Why do you need them?"

As the Arch Duke plants the demolition packs on the research lab's support beams, David replies, "We have to destroy this research lab, or the Congs can use it to create another atomic bomb."

Once the Arch Duke is finished planting the demolition packs and setting the timers, he says, "Okay everyone, grab part of that bomb and follow David."

So the knights grab the bomb and head for the entrance to the underground tunnel. When they reach the entrance, they hear the KABOOM of the demolition packs as they explode. The knights enter the underground tunnel, and soon they are within the cave. As they traveled through the cave, they notice that its walls are lined with crystal deposits that shimmer and sparkle as they pass. The cave is so beautiful that the knights almost forget that they are carrying a weapon of mass destruction. They reach a precipice overlooking a five-mile hole in the earth. The hole is sprinkled with gold and silver deposits, and looks almost as beautiful as the tunnel they have just come through.

The knights are so preoccupied with the natural beauty, that they have no idea that the explosion in the lab has activated a fifteen-foot tall sentry bot. This mega bot has been quietly sneaking up on them. They don't notice the bot until it grabs the atom bomb away from them, activates it, and straps it to his back.

The knights immediately draw their weapons and attack the bot. Some of the knights rush it with their blades, while others throw laser disks at it. But before any of the weapons reach the mega bot, the bot activates a level ten barrier field around itself. None of the weapons can penetrate the field, and the mega bot begins to shoot at the knights.

The Arch Duke says, "Stop attacking. Use your blades to block its shots." Then the Arch Duke turns to David and asks, "How could the Congs have built a bot with so much power?"

David says, "They couldn't. The bot must be drawing its energy from the atom bomb. He's using it as a reactor."

The Arch Duke says, "If that's true and we destroy the bot, the bomb will explode."

Then the Arch Duke tells David, "Give me your blade."

David does as he's told. Then the Arch Duke gives David the Duke's Blade. The Duke's Blade is a special energy blade that only the arch dukes have been carrying for over 300 years. This blade is a symbol of an arch duke's title, similar to the crown that the Teutonic kings wear.

After the Arch Duke gives David the Dukes Blade, the Arch Duke says, "David, as you know, I have no son. That is why I chose you to carry on after me. I wanted to wait until you reached the age of wisdom to give you this, but it looks like I can wait no longer. My last order to you is to get the rest of these knights out of here."

David asserts, "I won't leave you to die!"

The Arch duke sternly tells David, "You will get the other knights out of here! That's an order." David turns away and tells the other knights to follow him out. Then the Arch Duke turns to face the mega bot.

As David nears the exit, he hears the Arch Duke say, "Lord, I've lived my life for You, and you have always given me all that I need. Please give me the strength to do what I must."

David stops for a second, and turns his head toward the Arch Duke. David sees the Arch Duke throw himself into the mega bot, knocking them both into the hole. David is about to run back to try to save his mentor, but he remembers the Arch Duke's order. David gets all the knights safely out of the cave. Immediately after they are safe, the bomb explodes and the cave collapses.

For years, the remnant left behind after Project Evacuation searches the destroyed building and the hole, but cannot find any sign of the Arch Duke. There isn't much left after an atomic explosion. Still, the explosion should have fused the Arch Duke's genetic code to some of the dirt and stone around the hole. If the Duke did survive, no Teutonic from that day to this one has ever reported seeing him.

Chapter 2: The Evacuation

Having destroyed the Cong's hypnotic rays and the technology they had stolen with the rays, the small group of Teutonic Knights returned to the Teutonic capital city. Soon they would use one of the inverted gateways to leave Earth for the rest of their lives. A general feeling of gloom overshadowed the knights as they thought about losing their home and the Arch Duke in the same day. All the Teutonic Knights felt the lose of the Arch Duke, who had always been more of a leader to the Teutonic Knights then a prominent figure in the political realm. However, none of the knights felt the loss as much as David. To David, the Arch Duke had been more than a leader. He had been a mentor and friend for over four years. Now David would not see the Arch Duke again, until they would be reunited in Heaven.

Although they had completed their mission, the small group of Teutonic Knights certainly didn't feel like victors as they began to ascend the hill overlooking their capital city. They would not be able to afford the luxury of grieving for much longer. For when they reached the top of the hill, they saw that the city was being besieged by the Congs' brainwashed hoard. It seemed as if there were warriors from every race encircling the city, and when they attacked, it looked like the waves of the ocean beating against the stone of a mountain. The shield grid, which protected the Teutonic capital, could normally have withstood the hordes' primitive weapons indefinitely. However, like the mountain weakening against the relentless pound of the waves, the shield grid was starting to fail under the sheer number of its assailants. The knights could already see small openings appearing and disappearing in the shield grid's field. The openings were only a few inches across, but in time they would enlarge, and the horde would break through.

The Teutonic Knights were overwhelmed and heartsick. The knowledge that at least they had stopped the Congs and would be able to avert a war against the Cong's victims had helped to comfort them, but now it seemed that their efforts and the loss of the Arch Duke had all been in vain. Some of the Teutonic Knights became enraged, and if left unchecked by the rest of the group, would have rushed to destroy as many of the invaders as possible. Other knights began to argue with each other. Some of the younger knights even started to wonder if God had abandoned them. David walked away from the other knights and sat down on the other side of the hill facing away from the site and the other knights.

The girl who had handed the demolition packs to the Arch Duke follows David and sits down beside him. She says, "The knights are overcome with despair. They need a leader to pull them together."

David responds, "Yes, but our leader is dead, and it's my fault."

The girl says, "It's not your fault. He ordered you to go, and to get the rest of us to safety. Even if you had stayed, what could you have done? Our weapons wouldn't have penetrated that bot's barrier field."

David replies, "That's not what I mean." David lets out a sigh and continues, "I was the one who investigated the Cong's research facility. I should have found that lab, and then we would have known about the atomic research before we went in. We would have had a better plan, and the Arch Duke would still be alive."

The girl responds, "The briefing I had, said that your mission was to investigate the Cong's hypnotic rays, not the entire research facility."

David says, "Yeah, I tried telling myself that, too, but the truth is that by the time the Congs led me to the research facility, I had already been investigating them for over four months. I was tired of being on reconnaissance. I just wanted to complete the mission and go home. We are supposed to do our work as unto the Lord, and I didn't. I should have completely explored that facility instead of only doing what was required of me. I failed in my responsibilities and the Arch Duke died because of it."

The girl is quiet for a moment, and then she responds, "Well, maybe you did fail in your responsibilities, but you can't change what has already happened. The only thing you can do is learn from your mistakes and not repeat them. Turn from your sins. You have a new responsibility. The Arch Duke named you as his successor. *You are in command.* You can either continue to wallow in self-pity, or you can rally these knights and make sure that the previous arch duke didn't die in vain."

The girl can see David's confidence return as he stands up and says, "You're right. I can't let him down again."

David begins to walk back to the other knights, and then he stops and turns back to the girl, asking, "Who are you, anyway?"

The girl catches up to David and answers, "My name is Zipporah." Then they both walk back to the other knights.

David sees the knights arguing and knows that he has to stop it, but he doesn't know what to say or do. He looks down at the Duke's Blade in his hands, then up to heaven and prays, "Lord, please help me." Then David feels the Holy Spirit moving on him.

David turns to his knights and says, "All right! We don't have time for this. Our capital city is under siege. We must prevent it from being overrun. There appears to be something wrong with the shield grid. We must find out what it is and form a plan. We might be outnumbered, but the Lord is on our side. He is always on the side of those who follow Him; those who represent truth, freedom, honesty, integrity and love. Now let's get into our city and ensure that the Congs do not get any technology that they could use to oppress the other races of this world once we are gone. We have destroyed their most important research facility. Our brethren have engaged the Cong warriors in a battle and if they were successful, as I believe they were, they were then able to destroy the rest of the Cong's technology. We will not let all the blood spilt today be spilt in vain. Now let's go!"

David's knights cheer. Then David uses his wrist communicator to open a secret passageway into the city. He points it at a lake and sends the signal. Huge hydraulic lifts raise the lake and reveal a large metal conduit ending near the heart of the city. The knights enter the conduit and close the passageway behind them. Then they rush to the conduit's other end.

Once they reach the exit, the knights head for the city's Security Consul Overview Tower to find out if they can repair the shield grid. As they rush to the S.C.O.T., the knights notice that the evacdroids are working on their fastest setting, disassembling and preparing entire skyscrapers for travel to the new capital planet within minutes. There is a feeling of haste throughout the whole city as the Teutonics desperately try to finish the evacuation before the shield grid's eminent collapse.

The knights reach the S.C.O.T. and hurry inside. They quickly arrive at the shield grid control room and enter it. David sees the city's security chief standing in the middle of the room watching the shield grid's power supply and consumption monitor. The monitor's display indicates a dangerously low power supply and a slightly but steadily increasing power consumption. The chief's look was as a captain who has done everything that he could to protect his ship against an incoming hurricane and realizes it was insufficient, so he prays and waits for the storm.

David goes over to the chief and says, "Teutonic Knights reporting for city defense."

The chief quickly turns toward David and the rest of the small group of Teutonic Knights. As he sees them, a glimmer of hope returns to the chief's face. The chief replies, "You are an answer to prayer."

David asks, "What has happened?"

The chief responds, "After our main force of Teutonic Knights defeated the Cong army, destroyed their technology, and captured and imprisoned their scientists, the Cong leaders summoned up all the people who they had deceived. Then they planned an attack upon this city to try to steal some of our technology, thereby hoping to retain an upper hand over most of the races left on this planet.

By the time the Congs began their attack, all the other Teutonic Knights had already gone through the city's inverted gateways to oversee the reconstruction of our capital on Brotherhood. Before we were under attack and able to activate the shield grid, the Congs got a wave of invaders into the city. These invaders wore packs of black powder all over their bodies and went into our Interplanetary Communications Tower and our power plants and blew themselves up. The tactic was so completely unexpected that these "Homicide Bombers" destroyed our I.C.T. and most of our power plants before we could stop them. By destroying so many of our power planets, the invaders prevented us from being able to sustain a complete shield around the city. After a few minutes, microscopic, randomized openings in the shield grid began to appear. With our power supply already insufficient to complete the shield, even the primitive weapons that the invaders were using caused the openings to become larger and more frequent.

"We can't even get help, because without our I.C.T. we can't contact Brotherhood. Even if we could contact those who already evacuated to Brotherhood, the inverted gateways on Brotherhood aren't finished. And due to their complexity, cannot be finished for several more hours. Because it took your group so much longer to return than expected, we believed that you had either been captured or killed. Until you showed up, we had practically no chance of survival."

David asks, "So we're outnumbered and cut off. How much longer will the shield grid hold out?"

The chief answers, "We have about forty minutes before the fluctuations become large enough to cause a complete cascade failure, but the fluctuations will become large enough for the invaders to begin sending squads through ten minutes before the cascade failure."

David says, "So we have around thirty minutes before we get overwhelmed by invaders. How long do you need to complete the evacuation?"

The chief replies, "We're evacuating the city as fast as possible, but we still need about forty-five minutes for the rest of the citizens to make it through the inverted gateways, and an additional twenty minutes for our evacdroids to finish disassembling and storing our buildings unto the Hopeful."

David asks, "Are you sure that there is no way to supply enough power to the shield grid to sustain it at least long enough to finish evacuating the citizens? We can demolish whatever buildings are left, after we have all the citizens safely out."

The chief answers, "We've been trying to figure out a way to keep the shield grid up longer for the last hour and a half. Trust me, everything that could be done to strengthen the shield or speed up the evacuation has been done. We simply don't have enough power to sustain a shield this large for more than another forty minutes."

Adino says, "Well, then reduce the size of the shield."

The chief asks, "How? We have to use the emitters that are already in place. We certainly don't have time to make and setup new ones."

Adino replies, "Deactivate section five through seven. Those sections guard the valley entrance to the city. We should be able to defend them from the invaders. By deactivating three sections, we should be able to generate a complete shield for the seven remaining sections. Without the fluctuation, the shield grid will not require nearly as much power to sustain it. So by deactivating three sections, we'll gain about twenty-five additional minutes of shield protection."

Zipporah protests Adino's plan, and says, "We are Teutonic Knights and are sworn to protect the weak and free the oppressed. We cannot simply kill these invaders. They are not attacking us of their own initiative. They are being forced to do it by the oppressive Congs and their brainwashing. Killing them would be wrong and would disgrace the entire Teutonic Knight organization."

Adino responds, "So we should let these deceived invaders break into the city, massacre our men, women, and children, and steal enough of our technology to subjugate the rest of the nations of this planet, thereby making all our efforts to protect them, even the abandoning of our home, in vain? Would that be right?"

Zipporah says, "No, but there must be a better way to stop the deceived masses than by killing them. We just need to take time to think."

Adino replies, "Lack of time is at the heart of our problem. Every second we waste in talk and discussion, or even in thought, lessens our chances for victory. We have to move now!"

One of the other knights says, "Quit fighting, you two. David is in charge. It's David's decision."

All the Teutonic Knights looked to David, but he didn't know what to say. He realizes that they need to protect the Teutonic citizens and prevent the Congs from getting hold of any Teutonic technology, but he cannot think of killing people who have done nothing wrong, save allowing themselves to be deceived. David does the only thing that he can.

He tilts his head up, closes his eyes, and whispers, "Lord, I do not know what I should say to these knights. But you know everything and have a plan for everything, so please tell me what we should do and we will do it."

David waits for the Lord to tell him what to do, and after a few seconds, David receives the answer to his prayer. David whispers, "Thank you, Lord." Then David opens his eyes, looks at the chief and asks, "Have the weapon crates gone through the inverted gateway yet?"

The chief replies, "No, they were one of the last things scheduled for departure."

David tells the chief, "Wait five minutes, then power down sections five, six, and seven. Once those sections are down, get everyone through the inverted gateways and plant remote heavy demolition packs throughout the city. We can't leave anything for the Congs to plunder." Next, David turns to his knights and says, "Follow me. We don't have much time."

Zipporah asks David, "Are we really going to kill these people?"

David replies, "No. The Lord has shown me a way for us to accomplish our purpose without having to kill anyone."

Zipporah asks, "How?"

David says, "I'll explain it once we get the weapons we need. We are too pressed for time right now."

The knights run out of the shield grid control room. Then they quickly exit the S.C.O.T., and dash toward the grounds of city's central inverted gateway. Since the grounds of the city's central inverted gateway are only a few blocks from the S.C.O.T., it doesn't take the knights long to reach them.

Once there, David picks out two knights and tells them, "Go to the inverted gateway and tell whoever's overseeing the evacuation to stop sending people through the inverted gateway. Have them change the inverted gateway's arrival point to the center of the shield grid's sixth section and wait until we've gone through before setting the arrival point back to Brotherhood and resuming the evacuation. After you've delivered the order, rejoin the rest of us. We'll be in this inverted gateway's outgoing supplies warehouse."

One of the two knights says, "Yes, sir." Then the two rush to complete their orders. David, Adino, and the rest of the small group of Teutonic Knights head to the outgoing supplies warehouse.

Once the knights enter the warehouse, David begins to open the weapon crates. David opens seven crates and then pushes them away, but when he opens the eighth crate, he says, "Yes!"

David pulls out one of the weapons. A look of surprise crosses the knight's faces, and one of them says, "A Teutonic Stasis Hand Cannon? Those aren't military weapons. They're the standard side arm of city security officers. What are we going to do with those?"

David responds, "City security officers use these because they freeze suspects in time, without harming them."

Adino replies, "I see. Instead of having to kill the invaders who attack us, we can just freeze them. Right?"

David answers, "Right."

Zipporah says, "But the temporal stasis only lasts a couple of minutes."

David replies, "Under normal circumstances, yes, but if we take off the weapon's casing and rotate the temporal particle flow regulator, we can make the temporal stasis last for hours or even days. We'll use up the weapon's power faster, but if we bring some spare ammo canisters we should be able to outlast the evacuation time."

The two knights who were sent to have the inverted gateway reset return and join the rest of the group. One of them says, "The inverted gateway is ready."

David responds, "Good. Everyone take a Teutonic Stasis Hand Cannon, remove the weapon's casing, and rotate the temporal particle flow regulator by a quarter of a turn to the left, and re-attach the casing. Grab as many spare ammo canisters as you can carry and lets go through the inverted gateway."

The Teutonic Knights do as they're told, but the two who were sent to have the inverted gateway reset lean over to Zipporah and ask her why they are modifying the Teutonic Stasis Hand Cannon. Zipporah responds by telling the other knights what David had said.

Due to the fact that the weapons' casings were easy to remove and re-attach, and that the temporal particle flow regulator was clearly marked, the knights quickly finished the alteration and headed through the inverted gateway.

Once through the inverted gateway, David separates the group into three units. David tells Adino, "You're in charge of team one. Take eight knights and go defend section five."

Adino selects eight knights and heads off. Then David turns to Zipporah and says, "You are in charge of team three. Take eight knights and go to defend section seven."

Zipporah replies, "I am only beginning the third year of my studies. There are several here who have already completed their fourth year and are soon to be assigned to a Teutonic Knight division. Wouldn't you rather have one of them lead the third team?"

David responds, "I chose you to lead the third team, because that is what the Lord told me to do." David briefly looks down at his new blade, and then continues, "God seems to have His own way of judging whether or not we are ready."

Then Zipporah replies, "Yes, sir."

She selects eight knights and heads to section seven. David and the remaining seven knights stay to guard section six. A minute later, the three sections' shields drop. Soon the invaders begin to pour into the valley. Since the Teutonic Stasis Hand Cannons have a much greater range than the spears, arrows, stones and the various other missiles used by the invaders, the Teutonic Knights are able to freeze many invaders before they got close enough to threaten the knights. After a few minutes, the invaders got close enough to begin showering the knights with barrage after barrage of missiles. The light Teutonic armored vests and helmets that Teutonic students and squires wear to help protect them from small laser fire easily kept the primitive missiles out of their heads, chests, stomachs and backs. However, because the knight's, arms, hands, legs, and feet remained unprotected, the knights were forced to seek cover. Luckily, boulders and large trees were plentiful in the valley and the knights were able to protect themselves. The invaders continued to advance. When a knight tried to poke out from his cover to freeze a few of the invaders, he was assaulted by waves of enemy missiles.

David uses his wrist communicator to contact the leaders of the other two groups, and asks, "How are you holding up?"

Zipporah replies, "We've taken cover and we're pinned down."

David says, "Same with us. Adino, how about you?"

Adino responds, "About the same; there's just too many of them."

David replies, "I know. Every time we freeze one, there's three more to take his place, and one of our knights gets wounded."

Adino says, "Attacking piecemeal isn't working. We have to consider a new strategy."

David asks, "What do you have in mind?"

Adino responds, "A coordinated group attack. We all come out from behind our cover and fire at once. We blanket the valley with temporal beams."

David replies, "You may be onto something, but the valley is too large. If only there was a way to spread out the temporal beams."

Zipporah says, "What about the energy focusing lenses in our energy blades? If we removed and reversed them, couldn't they spread out the beams?"

David responds, "That could work! We would have to further increase the flow of temporal particles to compensate for the beam's expansion, but that shouldn't be a problem. Good idea, Zipporah."

Then David orders Adino and Zipporah to have their knights remove the energy focusing lenses from their energy blades, reverse the lenses, attach them to the end of the barrel of the Teutonic Stasis Hand Cannons, which will increase the temporal particle flow. Once this is done, the knights all come out from cover and fire at once.

The spread beams hit all invaders in the valley and froze them instantly. When more invaders entered the valley, the knights used the same tactics to freeze them, until the evacuation was completed.

Once the evacuation has completed, the knights went to the nearest inverted gateway. David activates the time delayed detpacks and the knights split into two factions. The first faction (consisting of David, Adino, Zipporah, and the other Teutonic Knights who are to travel to Brotherhood) goes through the inverted gateway. Then the other faction (composed of knights assigned to guard one of the remnant cities) resets the arrival coordinates to the remnant city. They walk through the inverted gateway just before the capital city is destroyed.

Once the first faction arrives on Brotherhood, they report the attack on the capital city and what was done to protect the citizens and ensure that no Teutonic technology fell into the Congs' hands. All the knights received special commendations for their services. The most senior knight in charge of the reconstruction took David, Adino and Zipporah aside and told them that he believed that they each have a bright future ahead of them.

Chapter 3: Fighter Training

A month has gone by since the Teutonics relocated. Today David and Josh are taking their assignment papers to the fighter registry. The knight behind the registry desk takes their passes, looks at them and says, "You boys must be pretty good to get Ace Squadron."

Josh respectfully responds, "Well, I think we can handle ourselves in a dog fight."

The man behind the desk replies, "That's good, with all the pirate activity we can use more good pilots."

The man gives Josh and David their passes, and they head to the training area. When they reach the training area, they see an old war bird (a veteran pilot who's survived many large battles) standing in front of the class. The old war bird says, "Take your seats."

Once everyone is seated, the man continues, "My name is Enoch, and my job is to take all of you hotshot cadets and turn you into Ace Squadron pilots. About thirty years ago, there was a young cadet who had trained for years to get assigned to Ace Squadron. When he finally did, he discovered that his training was only beginning. That young cadet was me. Now I've learned a few things over the last thirty years, and I'm going to pass them on to you. First of all, you all know that we are the best equipped squadron and only the most promising cadets get assigned here. Now let me tell you the reason why we get the best. We get the best because our assignments are the worst. If there is a job that all the other squadrons won't take or say can't be done, we take it and do it. Because our missions are so difficult, I will transfer out anyone who I don't think is performing at peak efficiency. Do you understand?"

The entire class loudly says, "We understand you, Sir!"

Enoch says, "Good, now let us begin." The floor behind Enoch opens up, and an impressive looking fighter rises up.

Then Enoch continues, "This is the Teutonic Crusader 120, the most advanced fighter we have. This is what those of you who make it through training will be flying. Looks impressive, doesn't it? Well, looks aren't important in a fighter. What is important is how it performs. Performance is where this little beauty shines. Its weapon system is nice, but nothing revolutionary. It has two energy canons, same as the T.C. 110, and sixteen homing nuke launchers—four more than its predecessor. The T.C. 120 is the first fighter to use a quantum drive instead of temporal. This is a 'good news-bad news' change. The good news is that you don't have to worry about temporal distortions when you use your 'faster than light travel.' This makes planning a trip much more predictable. You'll get where you're going when you're supposed to. More important is the fact that instead of draining your fighter's batteries when active, the quantum drive will actually recharge the fighter's energy system. You'll be able to outlast any of the pirate fighters, because when you run low on power, you can just activate the quantum drive, make a little light speed jump, and recharge your fighter in deep space. Anyone flying an old class fighter needs to dock his ship in a hangar and wait until it can be recharged by the station or carrier. Now, before you get too excited, let me tell you the bad news. The quantum drive is not as fast as the temporal one. A quantum drive maxes out at around five times light speed. The time distortions generated by a temporal drive makes it so that the farther one travels, the faster one goes. On extended trips, this can even make it so that a ship arrives at its new location before it departs from its last one. This means that if a battle is going badly, you will not be able to outrun the pirate ships. Your only option will be to outmaneuver them. With this in mind, the T.C. 120 has been equipped with vertical thrusters in addition to horizontal ones. This fighter has also been designed and equipped with the first spacial booster small enough to be placed on a fighter, instead of a gunboat. The booster will allow you to accelerate from a standstill to your fighter's top sub-light speed in less than two seconds. Special provisions have been made to protect the pilot during such rapid accelerations. With all these alterations, this fighter can outmaneuver and out-perform any other. Now that you know the specs of the fighter you will be using, are there any questions?"

Josh stands up. Enoch acknowledges Josh by tilting his head toward Josh. Josh asks, "I heard that the pirates modified some of their fighters with stealth devices. Has the T.C. 120s been equipped with them also?"

Enoch says, "No, but it does have quad spectrum scanning which will allow you to see the pirate ships even when they are using their stealth device." Josh thinks that he still would liked a stealth device.

If you can see the enemy, and they can't see you, you have a pretty big advantage. But if the new fighters didn't have stealth devices, there isn't much that he can do about it. So Josh sits back down.

Enoch continues, "Are there any other questions?"

One of the other cadets stands up. Enoch acknowledges him. The cadet says, "I know that the pirates are flying in our older class ships. How did they get them and what exactly do they have?"

Enoch answers, "The pirates got our ships by raiding, and subsequently taking over a number of our mothball stations. They scavenged the fighters they found and converted the stations themselves into repair bases. Most of their fighters range from T.C. 50 to 80s, but they do have a few T.C. 90s and 100s."

The cadet sat back down. Once again, Enoch asks if there are anymore questions. This time no one stands up. Enoch waits a little while, but the crowd is silent.

So Enoch concludes the briefing, "Okay, cadets, this is your first day and you may have the rest of the day to unpack and settle in. Tomorrow we start in on test runs. Whoever performs the best will be made your group leader. Class dismissed!"

Once the lecture was over, David took a walk around the station. It is a normal station composed of tri-alloy steel and guarded by a ten energy cannon torrent placed around the upper half of the station and an eight energy cannon torrent placed around the lower half. In the middle of the station, there is a ring that serves as the deflector field emitter. The station was built to accommodate Ace squadron's five fighter groups—the cadets, the first-year graduates, the second-year graduates, the veteran pilots, and the special missions group. Each group, other than the cadets, is composed of ten pilots and two stand-in pilots, just in case one of the pilots is unable to perform his or her duties.

When David is done walking around the station, he goes back to his room to unpack. The room is smaller than the one he had in the Knight's Palace, but it is right down the hall from Josh. When David is done unpacking, he goes to the pilot's lounge where he meets Josh. The two of them begin talking.

Josh says, "This is a pretty nice place."

David responds, "Yeah, it's nice."

Josh asks, "So why do you look so depressed?"

David answers, "I was just thinking about all of the friends that I've left behind."

Josh asks, "Still thinking about the Arch Duke?"

David answers, "Yes, but not just about him. I'm also thinking about my parents, Adino and John. They're not dead. They're just not here."

Josh replies, "You're sure to run into Adino and John at the annual knight's celebrations. You can still see your parents when you take your vacations, just like you've always done."

David responds, "Yeah, I guess you're right. I just need some time to adjust."

Josh sees that David is still depressed so he tries to cheer David up with a story from the past. Josh says "Hey, come on. Things aren't always as bad as they seem. Remember the time when you didn't think you'd ever see the Buskin brothers again?"

David replies, "Yeah. They both got new hover ships for their birthday, and they decided to show off a bit."

Josh chuckles and continues, "They kept doing harder and harder stunts, until they headed straight for each other and waited until they weren't more than five feet from each other before veering off."

David asks, "Remember what their mom, who unknown to them, was watching the whole thing, did after that trick?"

Josh laughs and answers, "Yeah, she grounded them for life."

David laughs, and then he says, "I remember thinking that I would never see them again."

Josh replies, "That's my point. You thought that you would never see them again, but when their mother calmed down, she lowered the sentence to a week. During the next week, they were able to come and play with us again."

Josh sees that he has cheered David up and quickly decides that it would be better to change the subject before David remembers that since he joined the Teutonic Knights, he has been too busy to spend much time with the Buskin brothers.

Josh says, "They sure gave us top-line fighters."

David reminds Josh, "They haven't given us anything yet. There are twenty cadets and only twelve of us are going to make it to first-year graduates. The other eight will be transferred to different squadrons."

Josh says, "Don't worry, I'm sure that we will make the cut."

David thinks about how Josh had been talking about becoming a veteran pilot as long as David could remember. There is no doubt about Josh being the best pilot that David had ever seen, but David never saw the other cadets in action. David really doesn't care too much about being a pilot, as long as he isn't stuck on reconnaissance. It would really be a disappointment to Josh, if Josh didn't become a veteran pilot.

David tells Josh, "I think that as long as we pay attention to what Enoch says and learn as much as we can, we'll do fine."

Josh replies, "Listen to you, still thinking like you're on reconnaissance. Everyone knows that great pilots are born with the talent to succeed, and I've got it."

David responds, "Even if you have raw talent, you still need to develop it. Don't get too cocky."

Josh replies, "I know. I'm just messing around." David smiles and then notices how late it is.

David says, "I better be getting back to my room." David pauses for a second, and then adds, "I'll need a good night's sleep if I'm going to become group leader tomorrow."

Josh smiles and replies, "No matter how much sleep you get, you'll never beat me."

David responds, "We'll see." David lets the game end and more solemnly continues, "And Josh?"

Josh turns and says, "Yes?"

David responds, "Thanks for cheering me up. You're a good friend."

The next morning, Enoch takes David, Josh, and the other cadets out for a test run in their new fighters. They go to the Grasite System.

Enoch says, "These controls are a little different than the training models you've flown, so let's run through them. You'll notice that the T.C. 120 is piloted through a dual joystick interface, instead of the single joystick with the point of view that its predecessors used. First, let's run through the simple controls. To increase the thrust coming out of the two main thrusters and make your fighter accelerate, push both sticks forward. To reverse the thrust and slow down or reverse your ship's movement, pull both sticks back. To increase the thrust coming out of your right thruster and turn your fighter left, push the right stick forward. To increase the thrust coming out of your left thruster and turn your fighter right, push the left stick forward. To execute a hairpin turn, push one stick forward and pull the other one back. Are you cadets clear on the basic controls?"

All the cadets responded, "Yes, sir."

Enoch continues, "Good, then let's run through the more advanced controls. To activate your right horizontal thrusters and staff left, push both sticks to the left. To activate your left horizontal thrusters and staff right, push both sticks to the right. To activate your lower vertical thrusters and ascend, pull both sticks away from each other. To activate your upper vertical thrusters and descend, push both sticks toward each other. Do you understand?"

All the cadets said, "Yes, sir."

Enoch finishes, "Okay, I have just activated your light beams, spacial boosters and dud missiles. Let's go through the weapons and evasive controls. The trigger fires your energy cannons, or in this case, your light beams. The top thumb button activates your spacial boost. The side thumb button fires your nuke missiles, or in this case, your dud missiles. The left and right pedals will bank your ship left or right. Stepping on the left pedal while holding the boost button and pushing the sticks forward will spin your ship horizontally clockwise. Stepping on the left pedal while holding the boost button and pulling the sticks back will spin your ship horizontally counterclockwise. Stepping on the right pedal while holding the boost button and pushing the sticks forward will spin your ship vertically clockwise. Stepping on the right pedal while holding the boost button and pulling the sticks back will spin your ship vertically counterclockwise. Do you cadets think that you have all of the controls down?"

All the cadets replied, "Yes, Sir."

Then Enoch says, "All right then, pick an enemy and let's begin the mock combat."

Josh asks, "Hey, David, do you think you can take me on?"

David sarcastically answers, "I'll give it my best shot." David fires on Josh, but Josh banks left and avoids David's shot.

Josh says, "You're going to pay for that."

David responds, "You'll have to catch me first."

Then David heads toward one of the moons orbiting Grasite 5. Josh says, "Oh, no, you don't," and takes off after David.

David reaches the moon, takes his fighter into one of its craters, and starts flying through the moon's network of underground tunnels. Josh follows.

Josh sees David and fires, but David executes a sharp turn and enters a different tunnel. Josh follows. Josh accelerates and begins to gain on David, but when Josh gets within weapons range, David activates his booster. Being in an enclosed space, the booster pushes Josh back as well as propelling David forward. Josh sees that in the enclosed space he can't catch David, so Josh turns his fighter left and enters another tunnel running parallel to David's. David looks back and when he doesn't see Josh, David starts to worry about him. David gets to the next intersection, turns left, and begins to take this tunnel back to where he last saw Josh. Suddenly, David sees Josh on his radar. David had gone into the same tunnel as Josh. David slows his fighter down and then sees a break in the top of the tunnel. David staffs up and enters the break, which leads to a new tunnel. Josh continues in the tunnel that he is in, until he reaches the same break. Then he rotates his ship vertically, passing through the break and continues to rotate his ship until he is completely upside down. Now Josh is going in the same direction as David. Josh rotates his ship horizontally until it is upright, and then fires. The light beams hit David's ship.

David says, "Good job, Josh, looks like you win."

Just then they hear a distress call from Enoch and the other cadets. Both cadets quickly head out of the maze of tunnels and find that the rest of their group is being attacked by pirates flying T.C. 80s! David and Josh rush to help.

On their way into the fray, Josh asks David, "How are we going to defeat these pirates? We're flying training crafts that don't have any real weapons."

David responds, "I guess we'll just have to outmaneuver them." David tells the other fighters to head into the rings orbiting Grasite 5.

The rings are made up of a combination of asteroids, gases, and spacial debris. The cadets enter the rings, and the pirates follow.

David has four pirates on his tail. He staffs right avoiding that asteroid, then left avoiding another, and then right, left, right; all the while dodging asteroids. The pirates are still on David's tail! He gets as close as he can to one of the larger asteroids, and then staffs straight up. The pirate ships, being only T.C. 80s and not equipped with vertical thrusters, try to pull up, but the two front ships slam into the asteroid. Only the back two pirate ships have enough space to safely maneuver through. David notices that another two of the pirates are following Josh.

David says, "Hey, Josh, how are you doing?"

Josh answers, "Not great. These pirates are pretty good! I'm having some trouble shaking them."

David slyly responds, "Remember the Buskin brothers?" Josh wonders what they have to do with anything and then remembers the conversation from the night before.

Josh grins and replies, "Yes. Why yes, I do."

Josh and David both speed up and head straight for each other. They get closer and closer, all the while enemy shots are careening past them. When there is barely ten feet from the bow of Josh's ship to the bow of David's, then Josh staffs up. David staffs down, and the pirates, unable to veer off in time, smash into each other.

Josh sees a pirate ship right on Enoch's tail. Josh heads toward them, gets right above the pirate ship, and pulls up while activating his booster. Josh is so close to the pirate ship that the boost pushes the pirate into one of the asteroids.

Enoch says, "Thanks, Josh, another minute and the pirate ship would have had me."

Josh responds, "No problem." Then Josh sees that the last pirate is on David's tail and David is accelerating toward a large asteroid. Josh thinks that one of the pirates must have shot out David's thrust stabilizer.

Josh says, "Don't worry, David, I'm on my way."

Josh rushes to help, but when David is not more than ten feet from the asteroid, Josh sees him execute a sharp turn. The pirate ship smashes into the asteroid. Josh says, "So, that's what you were doing."

David responds, "Yup, pretty good flying, huh?"

Josh replies, "Yeah, you're almost as good as me."

Josh and David hear Enoch say, "That's the last of them. Let's head home."

Chapter 4: Pirate Transfers

About a week after the pirates attacked Enoch's cadets, David and Josh, the new cadet group leaders, are called to Enoch's office.

When they enter Enoch's office he asks them to take a seat. Josh and David sit down and Enoch tells them why he called for them, "For the past couple of months, the pirate factions have been becoming much bolder. The attack against us, for example, was completely unprecedented. Sure, Ace Squadron pilots have been in fights with pirates often enough, but the pirates never before attacked us directly. The pirates would attack a fringe planet or a mining camp. Then we would send pilots to drive them off. More often than not, the pirates wouldn't even stick around. They would just grab whatever loot they could and run as soon as they saw us.

"After the House heard about the pirates' attack on us, they decided that they needed to know just what the pirates were planning. So the Teutonic security director came up with a plan to infiltrate the pirates and find out. The station administrator has asked me to pick my two best cadets for the job.

"When I saw how the two of you flew last week, I was impressed. You didn't have much experience, you were in a type of fighter that you had never been in before, and your weapon systems weren't even active, yet you both flew circles around the pirates. You are the two who I think are best suited for this infiltration assignment, but this is strictly a volunteer mission. If you don't want to go, you don't have to."

David replies, "It's not that we don't want to go. We're just a little confused."

Josh responds, "Yeah, this sounds more like a job for reconnaissance operatives than pilots."

Enoch says, "Someone from reconnaissance would not be suited for what we have in mind. We are planning to send two of our cadets to pose as pirate pilots."

David says, "We can't do that. You know that we are forbidden to lie."

Enoch replies, "I know. When the station administrator first told me that he wanted two of my cadets to infiltrate the pirate organization, I reminded him that since our pilots are Teutonic Knights, they cannot lie. He assured me that you would not be required to lie. The station administrator informed me that we have captured two pirates that were being transferred from one of their training camps to a carrier. The pirates don't know that we've captured these men."

Josh says, "I see, so we are to go in their place."

Enoch responds, "That is what the House wants. When the pirates see you coming in the transfers' ships, they will automatically assume that you are the two pilots they've been waiting for. You won't have to actually lie to anyone."

David asks, "But why does the station administrator want to use a couple of cadets for this mission?"

Enoch answers, "The station administrator wants two cadets, because the pirate carrier has a record of the transfers' ages. The older pilots just wouldn't be believable. In fact, the pirates we captured were actually a couple years younger than you two."

Josh says, "But they must know the pirates' names. I doubt that we have the same names, and as David said, we cannot lie."

Enoch responds, "The pirate carrier doesn't have a record of any of the pirates' true names. Their pilots like to hide their true identities even from each other. All the carrier record has is a list of its pilots' call signs. Since you two don't have call signs, we can give you the same ones."

Josh says, "All right, we'll take the mission."

Enoch responds, "Good to hear. I'm not fond of sending two of my cadets on such a dangerous mission, but I think you two should be able to handle it. David, your call sign is Sun Jumper and, Josh, yours will be Nebular Rider."

Enoch hands the cadets a data pad and then continues, "This will tell you the coordinates and time that the pirate carrier is supposed to pick up its two new pilots. You will find the pirate ships in hanger bay two. The clothes and side arms are inside the ships. May God be with you."

David and Josh say, "And with you." Then they leave Enoch's office to set out on their mission.

David and Josh reach the location at the specified time, but there doesn't seem to be anything there. The two pilots begin to wait. Around twenty minutes pass before Josh finally asks, "Do you think that we have the wrong coordinates?"

David unsurely answers, "I don't think so."

Just then, a ship measuring over a mile long, a half-mile wide, and 500-feet high appears. The ship is almost as black as the empty space around it. Across its side the words "Black Panther" are written in deep red letters. The ship looks more than a little imposing and a momentary twinge of fear grips the new transfers.

Josh, somewhat sheepishly, says, "I guess they were using a stealth device."

Being Teutonic Knights, their fear quickly passes as each reminds himself that his faith and trust is placed in the Almighty God. David's and Josh's holographic communicators activate, and the holographic projection says, "You may enter docking bay three."

One of the docking bays' doors open. David and Josh land their fighters inside. When David and Josh exit their fighters, a man tells them to follow him to the ship commander's office. David begins to wonder whether or not these pirates know who they really are. But Josh simply replies, "Lead the way."

When David and Josh arrive at the ship commander's office, the ship commander says, "Take a seat."

David and Josh sit down. Then the ship commander continues, "So, you are the new pirate pilots?"

Once again fear begins to grip David. He knows that saying yes would be a lie, but if he says no, he will both blow the mission and endanger Josh and himself. All the planning of his superiors and assurances that he wouldn't have to lie were suddenly undone by a simple question, not even a serious question, but just a bit of small talk. Suddenly, an idea comes to David.

He stands up and casually responds, "No, we are really Teutonic Knights sent here to spy on you."

Josh looks at his friend with utter surprise in his eyes. He was wondering what to do himself, but to just come out and admit that they were spies wasn't even something that Josh was considering.

Luckily, Josh's head is turned away from the ship commander hiding the look of shock on Josh's face from the commander's view. After a couple of seconds, which seemed a lot longer for the two knight-pilots turned pirate-spies, the ship commander chuckles and replies, "Good, I see you have a sense of humor. We can use that. But seriously, we Privateers are not like the Buccaneers. Eighty percent of what we make goes to help the staving families on our home planets in the Trysham system. So, if you are here because you're planning to get fat off of plunder, tell me now and I will transfer you to the Buccaneer's faction. We need pilots, but not ones who are only in this for themselves. With the Buccaneers, you can keep what you take." The ship commander laughs, and says, "Assuming, of course, that one of your buddies doesn't steal it from you."

Josh replies, "No, we are not here to get rich."

The ship commander smiles and responds, "Excellent, in that case, let me introduce you to your new wingmates. Nebular Rider, this is your wingmate, Side Blaster."

Side Blaster was a head shorter than the other pilots. He had red hair, green eyes and wore a roguish smile upon a face that couldn't have been fifteen yet.

Josh says, "Hi, pleased to meet you."

Side Blaster responds, "Same here."

David could tell that Side Blaster as well as the ship commander had friendly personalities. They didn't strike David as the lawless savages that he had believed all pirates to be.

The ship commander continued, "Sun Jumper, this is your wingmate, Fire Star."

Fire star was older than Side Blaster by at least three years. She had dark black hair and deep blue eyes. She didn't smile. Instead, she looked at her new wingmate the way a teacher who had been teaching for too long, might look at a new student on the first day of school. It was a cold, intimidating expression."

David still tried to be friendly. His reconnaissance training had taught him that the more that people liked you, the more they would let their guard down and the more you could find out from them.

David said, "Pleased to meet you."

Fire Star replied, "I wish I could say the same, but unfortunately, meeting you means that I have to break in a new wingmate."

Josh asks, "A new wingmate? What happened to your old one?"

Fire Star answers, "He got smashed into an asteroid in the Grasite system."

David replies, "I'm sorry to hear that."

Fire Star responds, "Don't be. It wasn't your fault. Besides, he wouldn't have gotten squashed if he hadn't been trying to be a hotshot."

David asks, "What do you mean?"

Fire Star replies, "He volunteered for a mission to try to capture some of the Teutonic Knight's new fighters. I must have told him a hundred times that only a fool volunteers for anything, but he just wouldn't listen."

Fire Star gives her new wingman an authoritative look as she continues, "When I tell you something, be smart and listen. Then you won't get killed, and I won't get stuck with another rookie."

The ship commander cut in, "It's late, and we've all had a long day. Since we don't have any more raids for today, and I'm sure that our new pilots would like to settle in, you are all free to go."

After Josh and David met their wingmates and the ship commander dismissed them, they headed to their quarters, searched it for bugs, unpacked, and discussed their mission.

Josh says, "This is a little strange. Here we are, two Teutonic fighter pilots wearing pirate clothes, armed with pirate weapons, and unpacking our things in a pirate room. Talk about setting a table in the presence of your enemy."

David jokingly replies, "What's so strange about that?"

Josh smiles and responds, "Well, when I signed up for the pilot tryouts, this is the last thing that I thought I'd be doing."

David replies, "Yes, I have got to admit that when I got assigned to Ace Squadron, I didn't think that I'd be going on a reconnaissance mission, but it's for the good of our people, so I can't do much complaining."

Josh says, "That sure was a close call in the office. It's amazing that you were able to fool the ship commander just by telling him the truth."

David responds, "Yes, but I feel kind of sorry that I had to trick him."

Josh asks, "Why?"

David answers, "I'm beginning to wonder if these pirates are as bad as we think. I mean, most of them seem pretty decent and if they give four-fifths of what they take to feed the poor, they're giving a lot more than most of our people."

Josh replies, "But our people don't steal what they get. They earn it."

David responds, "I didn't mean that what the pirates are doing is right. I simply meant that maybe they're not all bad. There are gray areas, you know. For example, what we're doing now is a gray area."

Josh asks, "What do you mean?"

David answers, "We are deceiving people who trust us and have welcomed us into their organization. We are acting in the best interests of our people, but I never feel right about spying on others. That's why I wanted to get out of reconnaissance."

Josh says, "I see what you mean. I never thought about it like that."

David gets up and starts to head out of the room. Josh asks, "Where are you going?"

David replies, "The faster we complete our mission, the faster we can stop this deception. I'm going to see what I can find out about these pirates. You had better stay here. It's late, and if the pirates saw you walking around the station, they might get suspicious."

Josh asks, "What about you? Don't you think that they would be just as suspicious if they saw you?"

David responds, "Probably, but they won't see me." David prays for God to hide him and then disappears from sight. Josh sees the door open and close as his friend walks out.

A few hours later, David returns. He begins to tell Josh about what he has learned. David tells Josh that the largest of the pirate factions is the Privateers, but the richest, by far, is the Buccaneers. Both factions are made up of people from colonies in the Trysham and Quanite systems. But, the Buccaneers are stealing to increase their personal wealth, while the Privateers are family members stealing to provide food, medicine and other necessities for their loved ones. Every colony in the Trysham and Quanite systems was a dismal failure. They are poor, underdeveloped, and starving. Apparently there is a strange gas present in the atmosphere of the planets in those systems. The gas is harmless to humans, but it prevents anything not native to the planet from growing. The money and materials from the Privateers are all that is keeping the citizens of those colonies from dying out completely.

David also learned that the pirates were not becoming bolder, but simply more desperate. When the Teutonic people relocated their capital, one of the House's main concerns was improving the quality of their space fleet. More money was funneled into the shipyards than ever before. Newer and better ships were practically pouring off the assembly lines and more knights were being sent to space flight school than any other training branch. The pirates were being hunted and captured more often. Less and less of their raids were successful. David would have continued talking with Josh, but just then Fire Star burst into their room. Fire Star heads to the room's intercom and shoves a small dagger through it. The intercom sparks and smokes as it short circuits.

Josh says, "What are you doing?!"

Fire Star replies, "We have to get you two out of here."

David asks, "Why?"

Fire Star answers, "The ship commander knows that you are Teutonic Knights. If you want to survive this mission, follow me and be quiet."

David and Josh follow Fire Star through the pirate ship. As they wind their way through the corridors, David whispers to Fire Star, "Why are you helping us?"

Fire Star replies, "My family was killed by a plague six months ago. I have no reason to stay a Privateer. I'm tired of living like a hunted animal. I figure that if I help you, you'll help me."

Josh asks, "Help you, how?"

Fire Star responds, "I want amnesty and an appointment as a Teutonic fighter pilot."

David replies, "When the House finds out that you left the pirates in order to help us escape, it shouldn't be too hard to get you a pardon. But a Teutonic pilot, I don't know about that."

Fire Star responds, "I'm not just leaving the pirates. I'm helping two spies escape. If I get caught, I'll be executed. I'm risking my life for you two."

Josh turns to David and says, "You could do it. You're the Arch Duke."

David had almost forgotten about that. Since the evacuation, he hadn't done much as the Arch Duke. David hadn't reached the age of wisdom yet, so he chose a proxy to vote on his behalf. As a pilot, he didn't have much reason to carry the Duke's Blade. He kept it on a shelf in his room. He was allowed to select up to ten knights as his personal bodyguards and anyone he chose would have to receive the same assignment as him, as well as the same fighter group.

David turns to Fire Star and replies, "All right, but first you'll have to pass the entrance exams and be accepted as a Teutonic Knight, before I can get you assigned as a fighter pilot. If you fail the exams, my hands are tied."

Fire Star responds, "That won't be a problem. I've never failed a test in my life. Now come, we're almost to launch bay three. I know the override codes that will get us out of here."

David, Josh, and Fire Star reach launch bay three. Fire Star enters the override code, but as the security doors open, David sees a small group of pirate security officers waiting for them. David shoots one of the security officers, and then ducks behind a storage container. Josh and Fire Star also take cover.

One of the security officers shoots at Josh. Josh dives to the left, and then fires. The security officer falls to the floor. Fire Star fires at a security officer, but he jumps out of the way. While in mid-air he fires back. The shot misses Fire Star, but bounces off a piece of reflective paneling and grazes the rope suspending a storage container above her head. Josh leaps toward Fire Star. He knocks her out of the way, but the container crushes her side arm.

Fire Star turns to Josh and says, "Thanks."

Then she runs up to the security officer who shot at her. She jumps up and kicks him in the face. The security officer falls, and Fire Star claims his side arm. Josh says, "Impressive."

Meanwhile, David finally gets a clear shot at the last security officer. David fires. The beam hits the last security officer, and the fight is over.

Fire Star says, "Good, now let's hurry."

David and Josh follow Fire Star into a gunboat with the name Street Brawler written across the side. When they get into the ship, Fire Star tells Josh to man the turret. Josh does as he's told. David watches Fire Star lean over the pilot's seat and plot a course toward Teutonic space. Then Fire Star tells David to take the pilot controls.

David protests, "I'm not trained to pilot a gunboat."

Fire Star replies, "I can't input the emergency launch code and pilot the ship."

David responds, "Okay, what do the controls do?"

Fire Star answers, "It's simple. The joystick controls normal flight. The point of view hat controls the lateral and horizontal thrusters. The index trigger fires the energy cannons. The top thumb button activates the boosters. The side thumb button activates the holding beam. The pinky trigger fires your G missiles."

David says, "Okay."

Fire Star takes her position as computer technician. She activates the ship's power and enters the emergency launch code. David tries to hold the ship steady until the bay door opens. He accidentally smashes into a few storage containers while getting his bearings. Then the bay door opens and Street Brawler flies out. She heads for friendly space, but the Privateer carrier sends four fighter groups to intercept her. David and Josh begin to shoot at the enemy fighters.

Josh says, "There are too many of them."

Fire Star tells Josh, "I'm charging the temporal drive." Then she turns to David and says, "Don't fire your G missiles until the temporal drive is done charging."

David asks Fire Star, "Why not?"

Fire Star says, "Because if you launch them at the same time that I activate the temporal drive, the gravitational disruption will keep the Privateers from tracking our course.

Josh yells, "Every time I shoot one, two more take his place."

David tells Josh, "Just concentrate on taking them out one at a time."

Fire Star says, "It's almost charged."

David tells Josh, "Just keep it together a little bit longer."

The temporal drive finally powers up. Fire Star tells David to fire his G missiles. The G missiles create a very small quantum singularity. The quantum singularity quickly sucks in everything within range. The pirate fighters try to veer off, but not all of them make it. After two seconds, the quantum singularity destabilizes and propels out everything that it has sucked in and destroyed. The remaining fighters are assaulted by debris from the ships that were sucked into the singularity. The debris destroys some of the remaining fighters and badly damages the others.

David, Josh and Fire Star don't see any of this. The Street Brawler entered temporal flux at the same moment that David fired the G missiles. The gravitational disruption covers the Street Brawler's tracks as planned. The trio is safely on their way to Teutonic space."

Josh enters the cockpit and says, "I'm glad that's over."

David responds, "Yeah, me, too, but one thing still bothers me."

Josh asks, "What's that?"

David replies, "How did the ship commander know that we were Teutonic Knights? We checked the room for bugs before we started talking."

Fire Star answers, "You two have a lot to learn. The equipment you knights use to check for bugs searches for a transmission device. In a ship that is already equipped with an intercom, all you have to do to listen in on the other rooms is to run a couple of extra wires so that you can activate the intercom's listening device. It's a simple procedure. Because the only transmitters involved are a couple of wires and wires are already running through the ship, you can't detect them. In order to use the extra wires, the intercom itself must be opened and inspected. All new transfers are placed in rooms like yours. The ship commander uses them to screen new pilots. Of course, he doesn't usually find out much that way. Most of the time, the pirates check the intercoms as soon as they enter the rooms."

Josh asks, "If the ship commander knew we were Teutonic Knights right away, why did he wait a couple of hours before he did anything?"

Fire Star replies, "The ship commander was trying to decide what to do. It isn't every day that we have Teutonic Knights in our ships. He was trying to decide between killing you, trying to capture you to ransom you back to the Teutonics, or feeding you false information before letting you go. After two hours, he finally decided to play it safe and have you executed."

David asks, "How do you know all this?"

Fire Star replies, "I was listening in on the ship commander while he was spying on you. I bugged his office a long time ago. He has jamming devices in his room and would have never fallen for the intercom trick, so I had to build a custom bug for the job. It cost me a lot of money and took me a lot of time, but it was worth it. I've heard about so many secret missions over the years, and I made sure that I was always in a position to get the best ones myself."

Fire Star lets out a laugh as she finishes, "Some of the other pilots even started rumors that I could read minds and tell the future."

Josh says, "You were spying on your commanding officer?"

Fire Star sees that Josh and David are very surprised by her admission, and she responds, "Don't look so shocked. You and your friend were spying on all of us."

Josh replies, "Good point. I guess we shouldn't be so quick to judge."

Fire Star responds, "No problem. I'm used to it, what with being a pirate and all."

David says, "Well, you're not a pirate anymore. Once we get back to Teutonic space, you can begin your life as a legitimate Teutonic citizen."

Josh responds, "About that, what's your name anyway? Teutonic pilots don't go around addressing each other by call signs. We only use call signs when we're communicating over an open channel or receiving orders via space transmission."

Fire Star hesitates. Josh laughs and continues, "Come on. You trusted us enough to place your future in our hands, but not enough to give us your name?"

Fire Star replies, "All right, my name is Esther."

Josh says, "Esther, it suits you."

While Josh and Esther talk, David says a quiet prayer, "Lord, you are a God of mercy and compassion. Please show favor to the fallen Privateers. They may have stolen and most have probably killed during some of their robberies. But what they did, they did for the sake of their starving and dying loved ones. I ask that you would look into their hearts and rest their souls. I also pray for those whom they leave behind. Lord, please take care of them, for we have removed their worldly providers. Also, Lord, I ask your forgiveness for Josh, Esther and myself. Please wash the blood of these Privateers from our hands. Finally, I ask that you will watch over Esther. She is about to embark on a totally different life than she has ever known. Please help her. Thank you, dear Lord God."

Chapter 5: The Highlander Station

The Street Brawler is on its way to Teutonic space. David is in the front of the cockpit watching a holographic recording of an old play. Josh is back at the ship's table with Esther. Josh has been using the flight back to Teutonic space to tutor Esther on the basics of the Teutonic Knights. They have been poring over the information that she will need to pass her entrance exams. David interrupts the study when he notices that one of the lights on the dash has begun to blink.

David says, "Uh, Esther? I think you better come over here."

Esther replies, "What did you do?"

David responds, "I didn't do anything. One of the lights just started to blink, and I don't know what it means."

Esther walks over to David and asks, "Which one?"

David points to a small blue light and asks, "Is it important?"

Esther replies, "Only if you don't want to drift though space for the next couple hundred years. That light monitors the ship's power. When it starts to blink it means that we are nearly out of energy."

Josh comes over to see what is going on and says, "So we just find a place to recharge our batteries. There are mining camps all over this area. It shouldn't be too hard."

Esther responds, "It's not that simple. This is a pirate ship. Miners tend to get a little jumpy when you land a pirate ship near them. Even if we can find a miner to deal with us, it wouldn't make too much difference. Pirate ships have been converted to run on Highlander fire crystals. We have to find a Highlander station or base in order to replace our crystals."

David asks, "Why did the Privateers do that? Highlander fire crystals are expensive and a lot more difficult to recharge than the batteries these ships come with?"

Esther answers, "Because, until they run out of power, the fire crystals put out nearly twice as much energy. The older pirate ships need that extra power to keep up with your newer Teutonic ones."

Josh responds, "Great, do we have enough energy to get us to a Highlander settlement?"

Esther looks at one of the holographic displays and replies, "I don't know. This gunboat must have been almost bone dry when we swiped it."

David asks, "So what do we do?"

Esther replies, "I'm going to search the navigation computer for the nearest Highlander anything. While I'm doing that, shut off everything that isn't absolutely essential."

After a few minutes, Esther says, "I think I've found a Highlander station that might be within range."

Josh replies, "Let's pray so."

Esther thinks that Josh is just saying that as an expression, until David actually prays, "May God help us make it to the refueling station. Lord, please multiply our remaining energy and stretch it out long enough for us to replace the fire crystals."

Josh says, "Amen."

After a brief pause, so does Esther.

The Lord blesses the trio and they make it to the Highlander station. When the Street Brawler docks at the Highlander station, Josh asks, "I'm just wondering, how are we going to pay for new crystals? Like David said, they are expensive, and we don't have much money."

Esther says, "We can always steal them."

David replies, "No, we cannot! We are Teutonic Knights. We don't steal."

Esther responds, "You stole that gunboat."

Josh cuts in, "Technically, we reclaimed it. That gunboat is Teutonic built. The pirates stole it, along with many other ships from one of our mothball stations. All we did was, *take it back*."

Esther says, "It must be nice to have an answer for everything."

David replies, "Stop. This isn't helping. We'll think of something. We know that the Lord will provide for us. Now, I'm hungry. Let's get something to eat while we figure this out. The trio starts walking away from the docking port. While they are walking though the station, a man grabs their money pouches as he runs past them. Josh takes off after the man. David and Esther follow. Josh is gaining on the man, but the man turns into a crowded corridor and Josh loses sight of him.

Esther says, "Now, what do we do? That guy just took off with the little bit of money we had. "

David replies, "Well, we could talk to station security. Maybe they know who he is or how to find him."

Esther responds, "I doubt they'll be much help, but I suppose we don't have any other choice."

The trio finds a security guard and tells him what happened. The guard asks them to describe the man. Josh replies, "He was about five and a half feet high. He had dirty black hair and only four fingers on his right hand."

The guard responds, "Four Finger Freddy. You can come and make a statement if you want, but don't hold out much hope of getting your money back. That guy's been a thief for years."

Josh replies, "He's been doing this for years? Why haven't you caught him?"

The guard says, "If someone's chasing him, he disappears into the lower sections."

Josh asks, "So, why don't you follow him down?"

The guard answers, "It's just not worth it for a simple thief. We only go down there in force. There is a lot of illegal activity in the lower sections and lone guards have a tendency to turn up dead. The place is packed with more people than any other part of the station, but *amazingly* there are never any witnesses. No. We only go down there to catch killers, drug dealers, and their ilk."

David gets an idea and asks, "Say, is there any reward for Freddy's capture?"

The guard replies, "Hold on a minute. I'll check."

He pulls out a small data pad, enters Freddy's name, and then continues, "Actually there is—fifty flames gems. It's a decent sum, but a little small as far as bounties go."

David responds, "Thank you. You've been most helpful." David turns and walks away. Esther and Josh follow him.

As the trio walks away, the guard says, "If you are planning on collecting the bounty, I need to warn you again that the lower levels are extremely dangerous. Don't go down there."

David turns to Esther and asks, "Would fifty flames gems be enough to buy the fire crystals?"

Esther replies, "Yes, but didn't you hear what the guard said? The lower levels are extremely dangerous."

David responds, "I heard him. That's why I'm going down there alone. I've been trained in infiltration and intelligence gathering. Don't worry about me. No one will even see me, unless I let them. While I'm looking for Freddy, I want you two to try to find another way to come up with the money we need. It never hurts to have a backup plan."

Josh and Esther look a little uneasy about David's plan, but they do agree to it. The trio splits up. David ducks behind a support beam, to keep from drawing attention to himself, and asks God to hide him. Once David is invisible, he heads into the lower sections. Josh and Esther split up while they look for another way to earn the money they need.

Once in the station's lower section, David begins to look and listen for any references about Freddy. David explores the lower levels for over an hour, before he finds his first clue. David hears someone mention Freddy's name. David looks and sees two men talking and eavesdrops on their conversation.

One of the men is quite large. He has muscles bulging from his upper body and a large scar running down one side on his face. The scar goes up through one of the man's eyes which seems to be milky white in color.

This man asks, "Does Freddy still owe you the ten flame gems?"

The other man is also a tight built individual, but he has nowhere near the bulk of the first. This second man replies, "Yes, but he promised that he would pay me back by the end of the day."

The first man responds, "He better. I'm running a loan office, not a charity."

The second man replies, "Don't worry. I'll get the money."

As the second man starts to walk away, the first says, "If he doesn't pay you back today, break his legs." David see the second man flinch, but the first man has already turned away and moved on too his next bit of business.

David figures that either Freddy will find this second man, or this second man will find Freddy. Either way, this man will lead David to Freddy, so David shadows him. David follows the man for three hours. Finally, the man finds Freddy walking out of a pawn shop, but Freddy sees the man and starts running down the corridor. The man and David both chase after Freddy. Of course,

Freddy only sees the one man chasing him, because David is still invisible. Freddy runs fast, ducking in and out of old, damp, and grungy corridors. Eventually, David sees the man lose track of Freddy as the man heads down the wrong corridor. David stays on Freddy's tail and begins to close in on his target. Just as David is about to grab Freddy, the man runs out a side corridor where the man had cut short the chase and slams his shoulder into Freddy.

Freddy falls to the floor. It takes just a second for Freddy to recover his wits. The man says, "Why did you run? Don't you know by now that it only makes things worse, when I catch you?"

Freddy tries to dash off again, but the man is too close. He grabs Freddy and holds him against one of the walls. Freddy's feet are off the ground, and the man's arm is underneath Freddy's chin. The man doesn't push with enough force to stop Freddy from breathing; just enough to make it difficult.

The man says, "Now, I need the money that you owe me."

Freddy replies, "Come on, Hennery. You know me. I'll get it. I just need a little more time."

Hennery responds, "I'm afraid that you just ran out of time. You see, Joe's my boss, and he's demanding that I bring him the money you owe. I'm sorry to do this to you, Freddy. We've been friends for a long time, but if I don't bring Joe the money or break your legs, he'll break mine. Now I can't risk you running, so I'm going to have to knock you out. Besides, it'll be easier on you this way. You won't feel a thing until you wake up." Hennery keeps one arm against Freddy's neck, while he pulls the other back, preparing to hit Freddy hard enough to knock him out.

David is about to intervene, but he is concerned that if he does, Freddy might get away. David can't stand idly by while Hennery breaks Freddy legs, because David has taken an oath to protect those who can't protect themselves.

Before David can act, Freddy exclaims, "I'll have the money. I just need an hour, maybe two." David sees Hennery lower his fist.

Hennery responds, "This had better not be a trick."

Freddy replies, "No trick. I've got a job, something big. I'll have the money before the day is over."

Hennery responds, "Do you think I'm a fool? No one would trust you with a big job." Hennery presses his arm a little further into Freddy's neck.

Freddy wheezes, "My part in the job is small, but the job is big and it pays well. I'll have the full ten flame gems today, I promise." Hennery lets Freddy down. Freddy coughs and gasps for breath.

Hennery says, "Okay. I'll tell you what I'm going to do. Because we're such good friends, I'm going to give you until midnight. When you have the money, come and give it to me. I'll be at home, waiting. But if you don't show up, the next time I catch you, I'll break your legs *and your arms*." Hennery turns and walks away.

As Hennery walks away, Freddy hollers, "Don't worry. You can count on me." Then Freddy gets up and mumbles, "You big jerk."

Freddy brushes as much of the filth off his clothes and out of his hair as he can. Then he begins to walk away. David follows him.

David knows that this would be the perfect time to grab Freddy, but David's curiosity gets the better of him. David wants to know just what this big job is, so he decides to shadow Freddy. Freddy winds his way into deeper and darker corridors. He continues to go ever deeper, until he reaches the very bowels of the station. It is there that he meets someone. A man who, David thinks, looks more sinister than any man he has run across so far.

The man has the look of one who deals in death. David looks into the man's eyes and sees the absence of feeling and of empathy, but the man is not an assassin. No, David can tell that this man lacks the intelligence and creativity that assassins pride themselves on. The man is a thug, an animal, who never shows remorse. His concern is only for himself—for the money and pleasure he gets from dominating and killing others. As the man speaks, David feels an unfamiliar contempt flow through him.

The man asks, "Did you bring the item?"

Freddy gulps and replies, "Yes, sir. One vial of catchatory venom straight from the Helping Hand, signed sealed and delivered."

Freddy hands over the vile as he continues, "Let me tell you, it wasn't easy sneaking aboard that medical ship. Especially, since they weren't staying docked for long. But when you give old Freddy a job, it gets done. Just curious, what's it for?"

The man says, "Shut your mouth. You ask too many questions."

Freddy submissively says, "Yes, sir." Then Freddy summons up what little courage he can and continues, "Sir, about my money."

The man gives Freddy a cold stare, but tosses him a small pouch. Freddy opens it up and looks inside. There are fifteen flame gems within. The man sees that Freddy is still there and says, "You have your money."

Freddy only nods yes. The man raises his voice and continues, "Leave!"

Freddy scampers away as fast as he can. David hates to let Freddy go, but he feels that he has to find out what is going on here. Catchatory venom is a narcotic stimulant and is used as an ingredient for many illegal substances. It can be used to make anything from drugs to poisons. It does have one legitimate use—as a cheap resuscitator. If injected directly into a stopped heart, it can jumpstart the heart causing it to begin beating again. Somehow, David doubts that resuscitation is what this man plans for the vial.

Of course, David could attack the man, knock him out, take the vial and then catch back up to Freddy. But David knows that that would only postpone whatever the plan is for the vial's contents. Sooner or later, this man can get hold of more Catchatory venom. No, David wants to find out just what is going on. He shadows the new man. The man leads David out of the depths of the station. In fact, David is nearly out of the lower section entirely, before the man walks into a dark corridor and meets with another person.

The new person looks like a military man. He is well built, but not at the expense of flexibility. David looks into this man's eyes and can tell that he, too, has taken lives. But with this man, the killing was different. He didn't kill for pleasure or money. No, his kills were on the battlefield. David could tell that this man was no saint, but he seemed to have a sense of duty. He had an honor that the other men, whom David had followed, lacked. David wondered what would bring such different people together.

This man says, "Oscar, you kept us waiting, and Mr. McDougal doesn't like to be kept waiting."

Oscar turns to the man who addressed him and answers, "Biff, I got the Catchatory venom that McDougal wanted."

Biff replies, "That's Mr. McDougal."

Oscar responds, "Whatever."

Biff sighs, and then presses his thumb against the fingerprint scanner next to a security door. The door opens. It would seem that Biff has a security clearance. He walks through the doorway and says, "Follow me."

Biff leads Oscar, and unknowingly, also David, through different security doors and passageways until they reach a small, but clean room in the station's middle section. There is one man waiting in the room.

The man is skinny, weak-jawed and has a nose that reminds David of a weasel. David looks at the man's eyes and can see the same lack of empathy as David saw in Oscar's eyes. But unlike Oscar, this man has intelligence and *ambition*. He was no mere thug. No, this man was a schemer. David had seen plenty like him among the Congs. This man is a coward who wants everything, but lacks the strength and leadership abilities to get anything. He is the kind of man who possesses only two talents, neither of which a decent man would claim. The first talent lays in his ability to twist laws and use politics, fears and prejudices to suit his plans. His second talent is that he cares for nothing but himself and his own selfish desires. David figures that this man must be the Mr. McDougal that Biff had mentioned.

Mr. McDougal says, "Well, Oscar, it sure took you long enough to get here."

Oscar replies, "So what? I'm here now, aren't I?"

Mr. McDougal turns to Biff and asks, "Were you followed?"

Biff answers, "No, I made sure of it."

Mr. McDougal responds, "Good. Now Oscar, bring me the venom."

Oscar reaches inside his pocket and pulls out the vial of Catchatory venom. Mr. McDougal tells Oscar to bring it to him.

Mr. McDougal takes the vial and says, "Here it is, the key to a count-ship for me! A little of this in William's medicine is all it will take. The venom will begin to interact with the Cong poison already in his blood. By tomorrow, he will be dead. The best part is that there is no way anyone will know that he was poisoned. The venom won't actually kill *dear, sweet* William. No, it will be out of his system long before he dies. All it will do is stimulate his heart to make it pump the Cong poison through his system fast enough to overcome his natural vitality and the medicine that he takes to overcome the Cong poison.. No matter what test they run on his body, they will still determine that the brave and once strong William has simply and *finally* succumbed to his old war injury. After his unfortunate and untimely death, I will take his place. I will be Count over all the eastern planets."

As McDougal comes down from his power high, he looks at Biff and continues, "And then, I will give you what you have always wanted—what William never would."

Biff eagerly replies, "A knighthood."

Mr. McDougal responds, "Yes." as he reaches into his pocket and pulls out a second vial.

This other vial contains William's medicine. David sees McDougal add a few drops of the Catchatory venom to the second vial. McDougal swishes it around, mixing the venom with the medicine.

Oscar sarcastically says, "I hate to interrupt, but what about the other half of my money?"

Mr. McDougal says, "Yes. Don't worry. You'll get what you have coming. " McDougal places the second vial back in his pocket, and then reaches inside his vest. McDougal pulls out a quietgun and squeezes the trigger.

McDougal shoots Oscar through the chest. David shutters at the needless death. Oscar was little more than a wild animal, but if David had known that he was going to be killed, David still would have tried to save him. Oscar should have stood trial for his crimes, and not been killed in cold blood. Clearly, McDougal had him killed, because he did not intend to leave any witnesses. David briefly wondered what that meant for Biff's future, once McDougal no longer needed him. David decided that it didn't matter. He wasn't about to let anyone else be murdered when he could prevent it.

McDougal hands the first vial to Biff and tells him, "Give this back to Oscar. Since he didn't get all of his money, it wouldn't be right for us to keep all the venom. Besides, station security may know about the theft, and they wouldn't think twice about finding a stolen and illegal substance on a known criminal's dead body."

David decides that he may need the Catchatory venom for evidence. Once Biff placed the vial into Oscar's pocket, David went to the body and removed it. David also finds twenty flame gems in Oscar's pocket. David takes them as well. Oscar won't need them anymore, and David still needs money to get the new fire crystals. Then David shadows Mr. McDougal and Biff.

It isn't long before they lead him out of the station's middle section and into the top one. The top section is much smaller than the middle or bottom ones, but it is lavishly decorated. The steel walls are covered in stone, as are the floors and ceilings. Colorful banners hang every where. David can hear soft music in the distance. Once when David was on Earth, the Arch Duke brought him to a meeting with a Highlander noble at the noble's castle. This part of the station resembled the Highlander's castle. As David continues to follow McDougal and Biff, the music grows louder, until they finally enter a large room where a man wearing the traditional garment of a Highlander noble is sitting. David thinks to himself that this man must be the Count who McDougal has destined to death. Two Crimson Knights, arguably the greatest warriors in the universe, stand guard—on the Count's left and right sides. Musicians and singers wait in the corner of the room for the Count's instruction. A young girl, David's age or perhaps a year younger, sits next to the Count. She is tenderly stroking the Count's arm. David can see a resemblance between the girl and the Count. She is most likely his daughter, but she could also be a niece, or even a much younger cousin.

David looks into the Count's eyes. David can tell that the Count is a wise and good man. David can see a great strength of spirit within the Count. The man reminds David of the Arch Duke. David senses the physical weakness of the Count and feels a deep sense of sympathy for him. He can almost feel the Cong poison flowing through the Count's body sapping nearly all his strength.

Mr. McDougal approaches the Count and says, "Is your wound any better today, my Grace?"

Count William replies, "Today, yesterday, and tomorrow, the wound is always the same. What need have I of days when nothing changes?"

The girl next to him responds, "Please don't talk like that. We must have hope. We must have faith that someone will find a cure."

The Count says, "Perhaps you are right, my sweet daughter, but it has been so long since I've felt strength in my arms, and so long since I've been able to walk without leaning on another."

The Count turns to McDougal and continues, "Do you have my medicine?"

Mr. McDougal pulls the vial from his pocket and replies, "Yes. It is right here, noble Count."

This is what David has been waiting for. He becomes visible as he grabs the traitor's arm and twists it back. McDougal crumbles to the floor. While still holding the arm, David places his foot on McDougal's back and holds him down.

William stands and shouts, "What is the meaning of this outrage?" The Crimson Knights draw their laser swords and prepare to attack David should he make another move or should the Count order it to be so.

William becomes dizzy as his heart pumps the poison through him faster. The girl sweetly says, "Father, remember your condition." She gently guides him back down.

David responds, "These men, Biff and McDougal, are plotting against your life."

William was taken aback by the statement. He never did completely trust McDougal. McDougal was always a little too humble. Respect was one thing, but the way McDougal acted around William bordered on self-abasement. McDougal seemed insincere, and William did not like the way that he looked at the Countess. William could see McDougal betraying him, but not Biff.

Biff had an excellent military record and had always behaved honorably. The only problem with Biff was his obsession with becoming a Crimson Knight. He just didn't understand that he was too old to join the Crimson Knights. Even if Biff's body could still handle the training, something that William had doubted, it took four years to complete the course. Crimson Knights, excluding those who died in the line of duty, averaged thirty years of service before retirement. Biff would be lucky to get ten.

However, the Count was intrigued by this young man. Even faced with four Crimson Knights, he held his ground. He didn't waver, and he didn't advance. He simply held McDougal down. William decided to give the man a chance to explain.

The Count asked, "Why do you believe this?"

David answered, "I am a Teutonic Knight. While God hid me from McDougal's and Biff's sight, I overheard their entire plan for your death and McDougal's intent to become Count."

David did not look like a Teutonic Knight to the Count or his court. He seemed too young and was wearing a pirate jumpsuit. But he had appeared out of nowhere, and William knew that some Teutonic Knights could become invisible. There was also technology that could bend light around a person and cause them to blend into the background.

William asked, "If you are a Teutonic Knight, then why are you dressed as a pirate?"

David answered, "That is a long story, but if you will allow me to speak, I will explain everything."

William couldn't see any harm in letting the young man tell his tale. William had the time. Although McDougal couldn't be very comfortable, as long as he remained still, he didn't seem to be in any pain.

The count responded, "You may speak."

David tells William the events that led him to this station. Then David recounts the story of searching the lower levels for Freddy, and how the search for Freddy led him to Oscar, then Oscar to Biff and McDougal. David tells the Count what he heard and saw concerning the plot to take the Count's life.

Once David is finished, William says, "This is truly a fantastic story, but do you have any proof of what you claim?"

David lets McDougal up, but quickly spins him around. Taking the Quietgun from his vest and the vial from his hand, David drops the gun. Using his foot, he slides it toward one of the Count's knights.

David replies, "You should be able to find Oscar's body where I said he died. I doubt that anyone has found or moved it yet. If you test McDougal's gun, you'll discover that it is the same one that shot Oscar."

McDougal responds, "I shot a brute that attacked me. Maybe it was this Oscar. I didn't catch his name when he tried to mug me."

David says, "He died behind security doors. How did he get in?"

McDougal replies, "I don't know. Maybe he paid one of the security guards to let him in."

David responds, "He paid one of the security guards to let him into an area that you just happened to be going though. That's pretty convenient."

William says, "Yes, it is."

McDougal replies, "Maybe he knew I was in there, somehow. I don't know, but it certainly isn't proof of any conspiracy, my great Count."

David pulls the vial of Catchatory venom from his pocket. He holds up both vials and says, "If you test the medicine that McDougal was giving to you, you'll find it has Catchatory venom in it. The chemical coding of the venom will prove that it came from the same lab as the rest of this venom."

David holds up the second vial and continues, "If you test the vial of Catchatory venom for fingerprints, you'll find plenty of evidence you need."

McDougal responds, "You won't find my fingerprints on that venom. I never touched it. There's nothing linking me to that vial."

David replies, "You and Biff wore gloves, but Freddy and Oscar didn't. The fingerprints of the man you killed are on the vial that the venom in the medicine came from."

William tells one of his knights, "I'm inclined to believe this young man. Have them tested. The medicine, the venom, the gun and the body—have all of them tested. And take McDougal and Biff into custody."

A panicked look crosses McDougal's face. As soon as one of the Count's knights comes to take McDougal away, McDougal grabs the knight's fire sword and stabs himself through the heart. Biff rushes to McDougal's side. When Biff sees that his leader is dead, Biff grabs the sword from McDougal's hand. The other knights ready their blades.

William asks, "Are you, also, going to kill yourself or do you intend to attack another?"

Biff answers, "No, McDougal took the coward's way out, but I will face my punishment. I may not have acted with honor, but at least I can die with it." Biff deactivates the sword and drops it.

William replies, "Well said, and die you shall, but not in a dungeon or on an executioner's block. You are brave. Such bravery shall not be wasted. You are reassigned to active military duty. You are demoted to private and a special letter will be sent with you. You will not be allowed to advance in rank. In battle, you will serve on the front lines. Perhaps through battle, you may reclaim some of the honor you lost when you conspired to kill me." William points to one of his knights and continues, "You get this traitor out of my sight."

Once Biff is escorted out, William turns to David and says, "You have done me a great service. How can I reward you?"

David answers, "I seek no reward, but if you are willing, I would like to pray for your healing."

William replies, "Go ahead."

David moves to William and places his hand over the shoulder were the wound is. David prays, "In the name of the Lord God, Jehovah, I command the toxin to be abolished from this man's system and the wound to be healed."

Williams' flesh burns under David's hand. When David removes his hand, smoke rises from the Count's shoulder. When the smoke clears, the wound is gone and the poison removed. William feels his old strength beginning to return to him.

William turns to David and says, "There are no words to express my gratitude. You have not only saved my life, you have restored my strength. Five years I have suffered the lingering effects of my wound. I have tried so many *cures* that I can't even remember them all. Everything failed. Then you come here and cure me in seconds. I can never repay you, but ask of me anything you will, up to half of my lands, and if it is within my power, I will give it to you.

David kindly answers, "I have done nothing. It was the Lord who revealed to me the plot against your life and the Lord who healed you from your wound. It is not lawful to accept rewards for what the Lord has done. I ask only that you remember the Lord God Jehovah and what He has done for you."

William responds, "Remember! I could never forget and I will tell others. From this day forward, I vow that I will follow your Lord and I will serve Him above all others."

After William finishes making his vow, David turns to leave the room. On his way out, the Count's daughter catches up to him and gives him a chaste kiss. David blushes.

The girl says, "That was for you. It wasn't for saving my father's life or healing him, because you said that you couldn't accept anything for your good deeds. But I gave you the kiss, because any man who has enough honor to turn down riches in order to faithfully serve his God, deserves at least a kiss. Maybe I will see you again some day."

Then she walks back to her father's side. As David begins to leave the room, the Count remembers that David doesn't have the security clearance to open the doors in the top section of the station, so the Count appoints one of his Crimson Knights to serve as David's escort.

David and his escort reach the middle section. The Crimson Knight is about to leave David to return to the Count, when they hear screaming and shouting not far away. They run to see what is going on. When they find the source of the commotion, they see that some of the station's security officers are in the process of breaking up a bar fight. One of the security officers is holding

Esther. David walks up to the officer and tells him to release her. The officer refuses and threatens to arrest David, if he doesn't get out of the way. When the officer sees the Crimson Knight coming over and getting involved as David's backup, the officer is quick to step down. He releases Esther and apologizes to David. David accepts the apology and thanks the Crimson Knight. The knight says that it wasn't a problem. He was glad to help, but now he must be getting back to the upper levels and the Count's service.

After the Crimson Knight leaves, David turns to Esther and says, "Do you want to tell me what that fight was about?"

Esther replies, "It was nothing important. Some men just can't stand losing to a woman. I did manage to get eight flame gems though. How did you do? Did you catch Freddy?"

David responds, "No, but I did find twenty flame gems. What do you think is the least that we will need to get out of here?"

Esther answers, "If we find someone who's willing to haggle, we might be able to get by with thirty-five."

David says, "Well then, let's find Josh and see if he managed to get some."

David and Esther begin to describe Josh to different people and ask if they have seen him. One of the men they talk with tells them that their friend sounds like the man who challenged Goliath in the Fighter's Pit. David and Esther get directions from the man and head to the Fighter's Pit. When they enter the room, they find that the Fighter's Pit is a low class lounge with a ring in the center. In the middle of the ring, they see Josh squaring off against a giant of a man.

Josh and his opponent are fighting with steel quarter staffs. David tries to rush to Josh's aid, but when he jumps over the fence separating the spectators from the ring, a man stops him and tells him that he can't interfere with the fight. David feels outraged. His best friend is fighting a man three times his size, and now this man tells David that he can't even help his friend. David just pushes the man aside as he continues toward the ring. Three of the fighters waiting their turn for the Fighter's Pit stop David by jumping on him. They surprise him and hoist him off the ground.

The fighters don't try to hurt David. They just hold him. David tries to break free, but he can't. Since David is unable to make contact with the ground, he can't get any leverage to fight. David looks for Esther and sees that two of the other fighters are holding her back. David can't do anything except watch and pray for Josh's safety.

Goliath swings his staff clockwise, but Josh blocks the blow. Then Goliath swings his staff counterclockwise. Again, Josh blocks the blow. Goliath tries to push the center of his staff into Josh's face. Josh blocks the blow with the center of his staff. Then Goliath gets mad. He grabs the back end of his staff. With his enormous strength, he thrusts the front end of his staff down. Luckily, Josh sidesteps the blow, and all Goliath accomplishes with this downward thrust is to sever one of the steel cables surrounding the ring. While Goliath recuperates from this unbelievable show of strength, Josh gets behind Goliath and hits him as hard as he can with one end of the staff, and then with the other. Goliath roars from the pain, turns around, grabs hold of Josh and throws him across the ring. Josh is startled and a little hurt. Quickly, he regains his senses and runs toward Goliath. Then pole vaulting himself through the air, he hits Goliath's chin with a flying kick. Goliath falls to the ground. Josh drops his staff and starts heading toward the ring's exit.

David yells, "Look out."

Josh quickly turns and sees Goliath lunge at him. So Josh drops down onto the floor and Goliath flies over the top of him. Then Josh rolls to where he dropped his staff, grabs it and the fight continues.

Josh rushes up to Goliath and tries to bring the end of his staff down on Goliath's head. But Goliath grabs the other end of the staff and begins swinging Josh around and around. Soon Josh realizes that he won't be able to hold onto his end of the staff. To prevent himself from getting too dizzy, he lets go. Josh goes flying though the air and is about to smash into one of the titanium posts that the steel cables are connected to. Josh quickly asks the Lord to protect him. Josh's body smacking into the titanium post should have broken half of the bones in his body, but the Lord did protect him. Goliath begins to charge at Josh, but Josh doesn't move until Goliath is right next to him. Then Josh leaps out of the way, and Goliath smashes into the post. When Goliath hits the post, the wind is knocked out of him. Josh sees this as his chance. He grabs the severed cable and wraps it around Goliath's body several times. When Goliath recovers, he cannot get free. The match is over. Josh walks out of the ring and joins David and Esther who are released.

As Josh approaches Esther, she nods her approval and says, "Impressive." Josh feels quite proud of his victory and the compliment from Esther. Then he feels someone slap the back of his head.

When Josh turns around, David yells, "What's wrong with you? Do you have a death wish, or did you just go insane?!" David sees that Josh feels hurt and is beginning to get mad. So David takes a deep breath, calms down, and asks Josh, "What would make you fight such a monstrous man?"

Josh quickly answers, "The manager offered ten flame gems to anyone who could beat Goliath. Esther and I were supposed to find a way to make some money, in case you couldn't capture Freddy. Remember?"

As Josh finishes talking, the man who David pushed aside earlier comes over and hands Josh a bag of ten flame gems. The man says, "That was great! Do you want to become a regular fighter, kid? I could make you a star, a real star!"

David responds, "Thanks, but the kid has to go."

The man replies, "I wasn't talking to you."

Josh says, "Actually, I do have to be going."

The man responds, "Well, if you ever change your mind, just let me know."

After the trio walk out of the Fighter's Pit, Josh asks David, "Did you capture Freddy?"

David answers, "No. He got away, but between your ten flame gems, Esther's eight, and my twenty we should have enough money to get out of here."

Esther cuts in, "Only if you let me do the haggling."

David and Josh hand Esther their flame gems and let her take the lead. Esther finds a fire crystal supplier and negotiates a deal that she can afford. Before long, the Street Brawler is ready to fly, and the trio is back on their way to Teutonic space.

Chapter 6: An Important Assignment

Two weeks have gone by since Josh and David returned from their infiltration mission. Esther is training to become a Teutonic fighter pilot. A stealth research team has been dispatched to one of the planets in the Trysham system. The team's mission is to analyze the strange gas in the planet's atmosphere and possibly discover a way to counteract it. As far as David is concerned, everything is going fine, so he is surprised when Enoch has him, and only him, summoned. While walking down the corridors that lead to Enoch's office, David wonders what could be wrong. Did he do something, or was this about Esther?

David remembers how on Esther's first day in training, a pilot made the mistake of saying that the pirates were, "Nothing but parasites draining the resources from civilized society." Before the pilot knew what had happened, he was laying face up on the floor, with a bloody lip.

David could swear that Esther got into more trouble than any Teutonic pilot he had ever heard of. But David had to admit that she was brilliant. She aced every test she was given. In a fighter, she could outmaneuver even her teachers. If it wasn't for her talent and high test scores, David had little doubt that she would have been kicked out of the academy. Teachers will overlook a lot when they think that they have a prodigy. As David reached Enoch's office, he had just about made up his mind that Esther was in trouble again.

Upon entering Enoch's office, David said, "You wanted to see me, sir?"

Enoch answers, "Yes. Take a seat."

David sits down and asks, "Esther has gotten herself into more trouble, hasn't she?"

Enoch answers, "Not as far as I know." David is puzzled. If this isn't about Esther, then he must have done something wrong. Enoch doesn't have individual cadets sent to his office without a good reason.

David asks, "Well then, have I done something wrong?"

Enoch responds, "Not that I know of. I asked you to come to my office, because I have a special job for you."

David laughs and replies, "Is that all? You had me worried for a minute."

Enoch says, "I am sorry to have worried you, but I don't know how you are going to feel about this assignment."

David responds, "Why, what's the mission?"

Enoch answers, "You are to pilot a gunboat that is taking a member of the royal family to a planet. I'm afraid that I don't know who the family member is or to which planet you are taking him or her. Everything about this mission is being kept very hush-hush."

David isn't too pleased about the mission so far. He doesn't like secret missions and he isn't crazy about ferrying a member of the royal family around. Quite a bit of animosity has built up between the royal family and the arch dukes over the years.

David asks, "Isn't there someone else who you can send on this mission?"

Enoch answers, "No, Ace Squadron has a reputation for having the best pilots, and this family member wants the best. You are one of the few pilots that we have with gunboat experience, and you got your experience under combat. There are only two other qualified pilots assigned to the station, and they are already on other missions. I know that the arch dukes and the royal family have been political rivals for quite awhile, but I need you to put that aside and think about the mission."

David replies, "The mission to take someone, we don't know who, to a planet, we don't know which one."

Enoch responds, "I dislike the secrecy as much as you, but if the royal family is personally involved in this mission, it must be an important one. The last mission was voluntary, but I'm afraid that this one isn't."

David says, "I guess that I don't have a choice." David lets out a sigh and then continues, "When should I start packing?"

Enoch replies, "I'm afraid that you won't be able to bring anything with you. You're taking a transfer pod and will barely be able to fit in the pod yourself. Everything that you need should be supplied when you get to wherever you're going."

David responds, "Why am I taking a transfer pod? Why not use the planet's inverted gateway?"

Enoch answers, "Because there is a computer record of the departure and arrival points of every inverted gateway jump, and the Teutonic Royal Guard has decided that they don't want to take the chance that the pirates could get ahold of that record. The pod should arrive within the hour."

David starts to protest, but Enoch simply says, "Dismissed." David leaves the office and waits for the pod.

When the transfer pod arrives, David steps into it and feels a little cramped. A transfer pod is basically a large storage box that has been equipped with a life support system, a level five deflector field, and a Temporal Drive. The transfer pods are remnants of the early years of Teutonic space travel, and they haven't been widely used since the invention of inverted gateways. The space inside of a transfer pod is barely large enough for a person to stand up in and you have to stand up. There are no seats, and the pod isn't wide enough to sit on the floor.

When the transfer pod reaches its destination and David steps out, he is surprised to be greeted by Adino.

Adino says, "Welcome to the Dove."

David turns and responds, "Adino! I didn't think I'd see you so soon. Maybe this mission won't be so bad after all."

Adino replies, "Won't be so bad. Do you know how many royal guards would jump at the chance to take this mission?"

David says, "That reminds me. Just what is this mission, and why all the secrecy?"

Adino replies, "The princess is taking some medicine, which we believe is capable of curing a deadly disease known as the Trynocn Flu, to Trynocn 7. The secrecy is because outside of you and me, the Princess isn't going to have any escorts."

David asks, "Why not just send a contingent of royal guards to escort her?"

Adino replies, "Trynocn 7 is not yet a formal member of the Teutonic Union. The House is worried that if the royal guard was to send a force large enough to protect the Princess, some of the citizens of Trynocn 7 might view it as an invasion. The House decided that a covert mission would be the best way to protect the Princess and avoid any problems with the Trynocn citizens."

David responds, "Why not simply send the medicine through an inverted gateway?"

Adino answers, "One of the chemicals in the medicine mutates when sent through an inverted gateway."

David says, "Okay, so the medicine has to be delivered, but why by the Princess?"

Adino replies, "Her farther caught the flu while he was there on a diplomatic mission. He hasn't felt well enough to return, and his daughter wants to bring him the medicine herself."

David responds, "Well, I understand what we're doing, but I fail to see why anyone would be excited about a delivery mission."

Adino begins to lead David down the corridor as he responds, "There are two reasons. First, if we bring the Trynocn citizens a medicine capable of curing their flu, they will be grateful. Trynocn 7 is a very wealthy planet and so their gratitude will be expressed with expensive gifts. The second reason is that the king is very sick and if this medicine indeed cures him, whoever helps to deliver it will gain a certain amount of royal favor for that help." David begins to chuckle.

Adino asks him, "What's so funny?"

David replies, "It's just too strange to hear you talking about gaining gifts and favor. The Adino that I remember was only interested with battle and victory."

Adino lets out a chuckle and then says, "Yea, I hadn't realized how different I must sound. I guess that when you're in the Teutonic Royal Guard you learn to play the politics." Adino sighs, and then he smiles and continues, "But don't be fooled. I'm still the best dueler around."

Adino slings his arm around David's neck and messes his short hair, just like an older brother would do. David laughs as Adino releases him, but shortly David's thoughts return to the fact that he is stuck on a small ship, with an annoying member of the royal family.

David says, "I am not interested in gifts or royal favor. I'm sorry, but I don't think that there is anything that would make me actually enjoy this mission."

Adino opens the doors to the cockpit. As David enters the cockpit, his breath is taken away. In the cockpit stands the most beautiful woman that David has ever seen. She has long, flowing blonde hair. Her lips are the color of scarlet, and her blue eyes seem to shine brighter than even the most flawless sapphires.

Adino says, "Princess Sarah, I'd like you to meet Arch Duke David. He is the Teutonic Knight that Ace Squadron station has sent to pilot this ship."

Sarah turns to David, and as he looks directly into her eyes, David perceives her kindness, compassion and godliness. In that moment, while staring into each other's eyes, David feels an eternity go by. Yet, when the glance is broken, David feels like it passed far too quickly.

Sarah softly says, "I am pleased to meet you."

David is so hypnotized by the sweet sound of her voice that it takes him a minute to recover. David thinks about what he should say to Sarah. "Will you marry me?" is the first thing that jumps out of David's heart, but he decides that that response would be too impulsive. David determines that before he makes a fool out of himself, he will find out how she feels about him.

So David merely smiles and responds, "I am pleased to meet you, as well."

Sarah asks, "Has Adino briefed you on the mission?"

David, almost lost in another world, answers only, "Yes."

Sarah is puzzled by the delay, and asks, "Is something the matter?"

Adino can see that David's mind is elsewhere. He tries to cover for his friend by gently slapping David's back and saying, "Don't worry, Princess. David is one of the best pilots in the galaxy. We'll get you to Trynocn 7 safely."

Sarah replies, "Well then, shouldn't we be going?"

David, brought back to the here and now by Adino's slap, answers, "Yes, of course."

David sits in the pilot's seat and plots the course to Trynocn 7. Sarah sits in the computer technician's seat. Adino sits down in one of the chairs by the table and straps himself in. The Dove enters Quantum flux and David, Adino and Sarah say a prayer for their safety. Once the ship has entered Quantum flux, it goes on autopilot and there isn't much that the three need to do for now, as long as nothing goes wrong, anyway. David, Adino and Sarah each find their own ways to pass the day.

As the day passes, David makes many excuses to be around Sarah, but he tries to keep from letting on that he likes her. He just happens to be hungry at the same time that she is. And David keeps needing to check equipment in the areas she's in, even though David is not sure what all of the equipment dose. As the day winds down, the three go to their rooms for the night. Sarah has her own room, while David and Adino share another.

Sarah is having trouble sleeping so she goes to the commissary for a glass of warm milk. She doesn't want to disturb the boys so she moves as quietly as she can. As she is preparing the milk, she overhears David and Adino whispering in the next room. Sarah can't quite make out what they're saying. She knows that it wouldn't be right to eavesdrop, but really wants to hear them.

"Should I put my ear to the wall, so I can hear better, or not?" she thinks to herself.

Normally she would not think of eavesdropping, but this was different. She decided that she really liked David the first time that their eyes met, but she was unsure how he felt about her. Sarah was well aware of the tension between the arch dukes and the royal family. She wasn't sure if it was possible that an arch duke could like her. David did seem to be spending a lot of time around her, but he always had an excuse and never tried to engage her in conversation. He might have liked her, or he might have just been keeping himself busy by performing maintenance on the ship. At last, Sarah's curiosity got the better of her, so she put her ear to the wall. She could now clearly hear what the boys were saying.

Adino says, "You like the Princess, don't you?"

Sarah silently prays, "Please, Lord, let him say yes."

David answers, "No."

Sarah feels her heart begin to break, but as David continues, "I don't just like her, I'm in love with her." Sarah's heart is quickly mended as it leaps with joy.

Sarah thanks the Lord and continues to listen. Adino says, "Love, don't you think you're jumping the gun a little? You've only known her for one day." Sarah wishes that Adino would just shut up and let David talk.

Then she hears David reply, "I fell in love with her the moment you introduced us and our eyes met. You remember when they taught us how to look through someone's eyes and see into their soul, don't you?"

Adino responds, "Yes. We were taught that technique for interrogations, but it takes minutes, sometimes even hours if the other person is well-trained at deception. You only made eye contact with Sarah for a few seconds. How could you have possibly broken through in that little time?"

David answers, "I didn't have to break through anything. Her stare was open and inviting." David paused for a moment as he considered that. He said, almost to himself, "It was almost like she was staring into my soul at the same time."

Sarah thinks about that, too. When David first looked at her, she felt strange and a little self-conscious, but that feeling quickly passed. As she continued to stare into David's eyes, she began to feel as if she had known him for a long time. It wasn't as though David, or anything about him, was familiar to her. She just suddenly felt like she knew who he was deep inside. He was trustworthy, courageous, passionate and reflective. She also saw that David was devoted to the Lord, perhaps more so than anyone else she had ever met. Maybe when David stared into her eyes, he initiated a form of spiritual contact, but it certainly wasn't a one-way exchange.

Sarah hears David continue, "The moment I looked into her eyes, I knew that she was the woman I wanted to spend the rest of my life with."

Sarah feels like dancing. She says to herself, "I can't believe it! I'm the woman he wants to spend the rest of his life with."

Sarah then hears Adino laugh and say, "Now, who's worried about royal favor? Seriously, why don't you just let her know how you feel?"

David replies, "Yeah, right, I suppose I could say, 'Listen, I know we just met, but I was wondering, if it doesn't seem to forward, will you marry me?' How do you think that would go over?"

Sarah smiled to herself as she thought, "You might just be surprised."

Adino says, "I didn't mean that you should propose. Try complimenting her. Talk to her. Ask her if she would like to have dinner together sometime."

David replies, "We had dinner together."

Adino responds, "Not saying a word to each other while you both eat a sandwich, isn't dinner together. It's just eating at the same table. Come on, man, show a little backbone."

David says, "It's not that simple. The arch dukes and the royal family have been at each other's throats for a hundred years. I can't just ask her out. I have to find out how she feels about me first."

Sarah thinks, "How stupid pride is. Here I was waiting for him to let me know how he felt, and he was doing the same for me. If I hadn't have had trouble getting to sleep, I might never have found out how he feels. Oh well, at least all I have to do now is find some way of letting him know how I feel. We could be married by the end of the month—well, maybe the end of next month. After all, Mom and I need some time to plan the wedding." Sarah is so happy, she feels as if she could fly, but then she hears Adino say something that firmly grounds her feet to the floor.

Adino says, "As much as I hate to add to your concerns, now that I think about it, you've got another problem."

David asks, "What?"

Adino continues, "Her father. As you pointed out, the royals and dukes aren't exactly friends. Her father would almost certainly disapprove of you two being together."

David responds, "The King may hate the arch dukes, but I'm sure that he loves Sarah. If she cares for me the same way I care for her, I can't see the King standing in the way of his own daughter's happiness."

Adino replies, "You don't know him as well as I have do. He won't see it as standing in the way of Sarah's happiness. He will see it as protecting his daughter from a distrustful enemy, and is likely to do every thing in his power to prevent a marriage between the two of you."

Sarah is shocked. She had never stopped to consider that her father might try to come between her and David, but she knows that Adino is right. Her father will not want her to marry, or even associate with an arch duke." David's response helps to reassure her.

David says, "I love her and if she loves me, then it is God's will that we be married. If God can create life from dust, move mountains, and bring the dead back to life, I am certain that *He* can change the heart of one man."

Adino replies, "Don't be so sure. Remember, God can move on a person's heart, but he cannot change it against their will. Even if God wants you to marry Sarah, he cannot force the king to allow it. In all things, the Lord grants us the freedom of choice."

David responds, "If Sarah loves me, I will find a way to marry her. No man, not even a king, will stop me."

Sarah took comfort in David's faith. She decided that she had done enough eavesdropping. She went back to her room to decide the best way to let David know that she loved him and to plan the best way to gain her father's approval.

Little more than an hour after returning to her room, Sarah is surprised by the combat alarm. She rushes to the cockpit.

When she gets there she asks, "What's happening?"

David answers, "We have just detected a Buccaneer cruiser and several groups of fighters coming toward us. We exited Quantum flux, so that we will be able to divert more power to our weapons and deflector fields."

Sarah says, "How could they have possibly found out about this mission?"

David responds, "They might not have."

Sarah is confused. If they are being attacked by pirates, the pirates must know about the mission. How else could the pirates have found them?

Sarah asks, "What do you mean?"

David answers, "Sometimes cruisers that don't have anything more profitable to do, will set up traps in order to catch potential targets. They activate their stealth devices, deploy spacial scanners, and lie in wait. We probably passed by one of the scanners. It did its job and scanned the Dove. When the pirates found out that this ship is equipped with an anti-scan shield, they became interested in it. Most likely, the pirates don't have any idea what or who is onboard. They simply figure that if it is valuable enough to have scan blockers, it's worth stealing."

Adino replies, "So, one of the devices that's supposed to be protecting us is what got us into this trouble. That's just great. Score another one for our fine people in the intelligence burrow."

Sarah asks, "Why haven't they fired on us yet?"

David answers, "If they don't know what we have onboard, they would rather not risk shooting at us. They might damage something valuable. They will wait until we are within communication range, and then they'll try to talk us into surrendering."

Adino asks, "How long do you think we have?"

David responds, "They're still pretty far off. They won't attack until we either try to get away or refuse to surrender. I've just cut our thrusters. We should have about ten minutes before we are within range of their antiquated communication gear."

Sarah says, "What if we just transfer all our power to our deflector fields and make a run for it? When we get past them, we can kick in our quantum drive and try to outrun them."

Adino answers, "The pirate ships are still using temporal drives. We can't outrun them. If we could, we wouldn't have exited quantum flux. We would have just diverted course. No. Our only chance is to get in close and throw everything we've got at them. If we get lucky, we might hit a vital system and cripple, or even destroy, their ship."

Sarah replies, "Do you have any idea how bad the odds are on a gunboat defeating a cruiser? That's like a sparrow trying to beat a falcon. "

David responds, "I think that I know how to take care of the cruiser. When I was abroad the Privateer carrier, I saw a diagram of one of these cruisers. And in order…"

Adino interrupts, "What? When were you aboard a Privateer carrier?"

David answers, "It's a long story. I'll tell you later. Now, back to what I was saying. In order to increase efficiency, the pirates tied all the main systems through a control hub right below the bridge. This control hub is protected by a level fifteen deflector field. But the field uses so much power that it requires its own separate mega battery. If we program one of our nukes to home in on the highest single unit power source on the pirate's ship, we should be able to destroy the field's mega battery. Once the cruiser's control hub becomes vulnerable, it'll withdraw. If a control hub is destroyed, the cruiser's entire computer system is totaled. It takes a lot of time to repair that kind of damage. I doubt that the Buccaneer captain will want to risk his ship being held up for that long, not to mention the cost of the repair work, for a ship that he doesn't know the value of. But I still don't know what to do about the fighters."

Sarah replies, "Leave them to me."

Adino asks, "Why? What are you going to do?"

Sarah smiles and responds, "It's a surprise, but don't worry. I know what I'm doing."

Adino replies, "Okay. David and I will program the nuke, while you do whatever you're going to do, to take care of the fighters."

About nine minutes after the trio began their work, they heard a beeping sound coming from the communications counsel.

Adino says, "We're not finished programming the nuke."

Sarah adds, "It will take at least five more minutes before I'm done."

David responds, "Okay, I'll try to stall them. You two keep working." David goes to the communication control counsel and activates the ship-to-ship radio transmitter.

The commander of the Buccaneer cruiser says, "Teutonic space ship, you are outnumbered and overpowered. Surrender at once, and we will spare your lives."

David responds, "Buccaneer attack cruiser, this is Teutonic space. You have no right to be here. If you do not leave this area, at once, you will be attacked."

David's response is just bold enough to make the Buccaneer captain nervous. The captain wonders whether the Teutonics are bluffing or if they have a trick up their sleeve. You don't get to be a Buccaneer captain unless you are careful not to risk more than you can afford to lose and not to risk anything unless there is something more valuable to be gained.

The Buccaneer captain cuts the communication and asks his intelligence officer, "Can you detect any other Teutonic ships in the area?"

The officer answers, "No, but I haven't used the spectral scanners to check for stealth ships."

The captain angrily asks, "Why not?"

The officer timidly replies, "Sir, the Teutonics don't have many ships with stealth fields. It didn't seem to be worth the extra time checking would have taken."

The captain responds, "Well, it certainly seems to be *worth it* now, doesn't it?"

The officer nods, and the captain continues, "Run a spectral analysis. Then get out of my sight. Helmsman, back us off until the analysis is complete. If our little gunboat does have friends, I want it to appear like we are complying with their demands."

The helmsman responds, "Yes, Sir." The pirate cruiser begins to back away from the Dove, and the fighters follow suit

David breathes a sigh of relief and hollers toward Adino who is in the back of the Dove working on the nuke, "How are you coming?"

Adino replies, "I'm almost done."

The pirate ships begin to move forward toward the Dove, and David responds, "Good, I don't think we have much time left."

The cruiser moves within communication range of the Dove and the captain tells David, "You are an idiot. Your ruse served only to waste both of our time."

David cuts in, "You may have wasted your time, but we haven't wasted ours. We fully intend to attack you, if you do not immediately vacate this area."

The Buccaneer captain laughs and responds, "You've got nerve, kid, but we've already scanned this section of space. There are no ships waiting to come and help you, and you don't stand a chance against us by yourself. Why don't you just surrender and save us the trouble of disabling your ship? I promise that you'll get better treatment, if you surrender."

David says, "As kind as your offer is, we will never surrender to the likes of you."

The Buccaneer commander responds, "Very well. Then we will just have to take you by force!" With that warning, the Buccaneer ships attack the lone Teutonic, Dove.

David asks Adino, "Are you done yet?"

Adino answers, "I just finished loading the nuke into the launcher. It's all ready."

David prays, "Lord, please let this work." Then he fires.

The nuke locks onto the mega battery and heads straight for it. When the nuke nears the mega battery, the cruiser's auto defense cannons begin to fire at it, but the nuke's tricreneum casing shields the nuke long enough for it to reach the target.

When the cruiser's damage officer reports that the control hub is vulnerable, the captain growls, but still orders the helmsman to take the ship out of the battle area. Before the pirate cruiser enters temporal flux, the captain promises a big reward to whomever of the fighter pilots manages to disable the Teutonic ship. The pirate fighters begin to attack the Dove with increased vigor.

As the Dove's deflectors begin to weaken, Sarah enters the cockpit and tells David, "I'm done making the adjustments. Get the ship out of here at the fastest sub-light speed that you can." David looks at Sarah with a questioning expression. He knows that there isn't anything that she could have done to enable the gunboat to outrun the pirate fighters.

Sarah sees his expression and continues, "I know we can't outrun them, but they have to be going extremely fast for this to work."

David says, "Okay." And the Dove flies away as fast as it can without entering Quantum flux. The pirate fighters follow.

Sarah says, "Press the holding beam button."

David replies, "Why? We want to get away from the fighters not bring them with us."

Sarah responds, "Trust me. And just in case this doesn't work, I want you to know that I know how you feel about me, and I feel the same way about you."

David replies, "You do?"

As Sarah nods her head. the Dove's deflector field begins to collapse. Sarah says, "But if you don't activate the holding beam right now, we are all in big trouble."

David presses the button. All the fighters are thrown back. They violently collide into each other and are either disabled or destroyed.

David asks Sarah, "How did you do that?"

Sarah answers, "I widened the holding beam and reversed its poles. When you activated it, it worked like a repulsive field. The enemy fighters were thrown back. Because of the velocity they were traveling at, the pilots weren't able to regain control over their fighters until it was too late."

David says, "You're incredible. Do you know that?"

Sarah smiles and replies, "Thank you. You're not bad yourself."

David smiles and responds, "Thank you."

Over the few days remaining on the trip to Trynocn 7, David and Sarah spend almost every waking moment together. They talk about anything and everything they can think of, including several conversations on what would be the best course of action to take with her father. Finally, they decide that the best thing would be for Sarah to stay by her father's side until he feels better. Then she should try to ease her father into a discussion about David.

Chapter 7: Trynocn 7

When the Dove lands on Trynocn 7 and David exits the Dove, Adino says, "Here it is, Trynocn 7 one of the most beautifully exotic planets in the galaxy!"

David is taken aback by the landscape around him. Except for the towering mountains that the Trynocn cities are built on, there is nothing but water as far as the eye can see. The water is not troubled like the oceans on earth with their waves roaring and dashing themselves against the rocks. No. These great lakes are peaceful and filled with fresh water that literally smells sweet. The only visible motion in the water that the trio can see is caused by several pairs of dolphin-like creatures leaping various heights out of the water, then doing flips or spins, before retuning to it.

David marvels at the beauty around him and at the graceful movements of the creatures. He is, however, quite startled when one of the dolphin-like creatures comes up to the trio and says, "Welcome, I'm Doulphla, of the Dauphlines. You care to join us in a swim?"

Sarah and Adino have been to this planet before, so they are not surprised by the talking Dauphline's appearance. But David, who has never seen any talking animals before, is dumbfounded and just stands there frozen stiff for a minute.

Sarah wants to get the medicine to her father as quickly as possible and replies, "I'm afraid that I can't go swimming right now."

Adino responds, "I'm going to have to wait, too. If I'm not with this lady when she delivers the medicine, I could get reprimanded."

Finally David regains his senses. He approaches Doulphla and responds, "You can speak?"

Doulphla answers, "Of course, I speak. If you're wondering how it is that you can understand my language, that is accomplished by my translating mouthpiece. A second translator placed by my ear allows me to understand you. Now, do you care to join us? It's great fun."

David replies, "I'm sorry, but I can't join you now. I've got to get this medicine to the hospital."

Doulphla responds, "Oh, that's too bad, but maybe you can join us later."

David says, "I would like that." Then David rushes to catch up to his companions, who by now are several yards ahead of him.

The trio enters the hospital lobby. While they are waiting for the hospital administrator to come, David notices that a small man who is wearing a white jacket is watching him. David is about to go over to the man and asks him if something is wrong. But before David can say anything, the hospital administrator comes up to the trio and says, "Thank you so much. The medicine has arrived just in time. Please, follow me."

David, Sarah and Adino follow the administrator to the quarantined room where Sarah's father is being kept. The hospital administrator goes into a closet and takes out a bio suite.

He hands it to Sarah and says, "I'm sure that you would like to see your father, so why don't you put this on and bring him some of this new wonder drug."

After Sarah goes to her farther, the hospital administrator continues, "Now, you boys must be hungry. We have prepared a banquet in honor of the brave Teutonics who have brought us a medicine to cure our deadly flu. Please, follow me." Adino begins to follow the hospital administrator, but then he notices that David isn't coming.

Adino goes over to David and says, "Aren't you going to come? The banquet's in your honor, too."

David replies, "I'll be there in a minute, but first, I've got something to take care of."

Adino responds, "Okay, I'll save you a seat." Then Adino follows the hospital administrator to the banquet.

David goes into the lobby. He sees that the short man is still there. David goes over to the man and says, "Excuse me, but did you want help with something?"

The short man responds, "Are you the Arch Duke?"

David answers, "Yes, I am."

Then the little man says, "Then I could use your help." The short man extends his hand as he continues, "My name is Zacchaeus."

David shakes Zacchaeus' hand and replies, "I'm Arch Duke David. How can I be of service?"

Zacchaeus answers, "You can come to my laboratory. I've got something that I think will be a great help to the Teutonic Knights."

David replies, "Lead the way."

When David enters the laboratory, he is amazed to see a giant, wolf-like creature flying around the room. The creature spots David and lands on one of the large stalagmites that are rising up from the floor.

David turns to Zacchaeus and asks, "What is that?"

Zacchaeus answers, "This is Grucharse. He is why I brought you here. Grucharse is a winged wolf."

David replies, "What do you mean by, 'He is why I brought you here?' I thought you said that you had something that would be a great help to the Teutonic knights."

Zacchaeus responds, "The winged wolves can be. They are approximately five times the size of a normal wolf. They have a forty-foot wingspan which allows them to fly or glide for great distances without resting. They are incredibly strong. They heal at a remarkable rate, and they are significantly smarter than even the brightest of their canine brethren."

David says, "That is very impressive, but although this planet may not have laws against genetic manipulation, the Teutonics do. The House would never let Teutonic Knights use these winged wolves."

Zacchaeus replies, "No one has tampered with their genetic structure. These creatures are the way that the Great Creator made them."

David asks, "If they haven't been genetically altered, why are they so different from any other form of canine?"

Zacchaeus replies, "Why is a house cat so different from a loin or a white tiger? Why are mice so different from skunks or bats? Just because something is different from the other members of its family doesn't mean that it's been genetically altered."

David responds, "You have a point, but I must be sure that you are telling the truth. Teutonic Knights can tell if a person is being honest by staring into the person's eyes. Are you willing to let me test you?"

Zacchaeus answers, "Go ahead. I have nothing to hide."

As David stares into the man's eyes, he can tell that Zacchaeus is being truthful. David says, "I am sorry that I didn't believe you, but among the Teutonics there are few crimes worse than genetic manipulation. I had to be sure that I wasn't going to get involved in anything illegal."

Zacchaeus replies, "That is all right. We have strict laws against genetic manipulation ourselves. If I were in your shoes, I would be wary as well. At least you're more open-minded then the King was."

David asks, "You have already talked with the King?"

Zacchaeus answers, "I tried to. First, I tried to get ahold of Debra, the current leader of the Teutonic knights, but she was too busy. She asked the king, who was already here, to come talk to me. As soon as he saw Grucharse, he got very upset and stormed out of the lab. I tried to catch up to him hoping that I would be able to talk with him, but he wouldn't believe that I didn't alter Grucharse's genes. Finally, the king got tired of my bugging him. He said that even if I wasn't using genetic manipulation, he didn't want any wild animals becoming Teutonic Knights."

David solemnly replies, "The King is against this."

David is not happy. He can see that the winged wolves could be an asset to the Teutonic Knights, but David really doesn't want to go against the King's wishes right now. David knows that opposing the king at this time is likely to make the king against a marriage between David and his daughter all the more. On the other hand, David is the Arch Duke. It is his responsibility to introduce positive changes for the Teutonic Knights and Teutonic citizens.

David sighs and then continues, "Are you sure that these winged wolves can be trusted?"

David is surprised when the winged wolf answers him, "We are very loyal and never deceive other beings."

David turns to Zacchaeus and whispers, "You could have told me that winged wolves can speak and understand our language."

Zacchaeus answers, "Normally they can't. Their native language is composed of growls, roars, and howls. I studied the translators that were made for the Dauphlines and found a way to adapt the technology for the winged wolves. That's what I've been working on in my lab. The large necklace and pendent around Grucharse's neck translates what we say into his language and what he says into ours."

David whispers, "I think that you had better tell me everything that you know about these winged wolves, before I stick my foot in my mouth again."

Zacchaeus responds, "Well, to start with, whispering doesn't do much good. Winged wolves have exceptional hearing."

David turns to Grucharse and sees that he is smiling. Then David turns back to Zacchaeus and asks, "Is there anything else that I should know?"

Zacchaeus answers, "Oh, yes. Winged wolves are remarkable creatures. They can stand on their hind legs leaving their fore legs to be used as arms. Their DNA is toxic to most species making their bite very deadly. They're omnivorous eating both meat and plants, but their digestion doesn't properly metabolize raw meat. Finally, they have an inborn resistance to most poisons."

David responds, "Wait. They can't metabolize raw meat? So how did they cook their food before humans came to this planet?"

Zacchaeus answers, "They have a thin membrane that they can deploy over their eyes. This membrane reflects and focuses light, similar to what a laser does. The winged wolves use this ability to spark a fire to cook the animals they kill."

David says, "That's amazing! I've never heard of any creature that could do that."

Zacchaeus replies, "As I said, 'Winged wolves are remarkable creatures.' That's why I came to you. I do believe that they would make a strong addition to the Teutonic Knights. But if the King is against it, I know that I won't be able to convince Debra by myself. So I started trying to get ahold of the Arch Duke. I figured who better to oppose the King, but I've had a hard time trying to track you down. It seems like you're never in one place for very long. It's the life of a Teutonic Knight, I suppose. I could hardly believe it when I saw you in the hospital. Talk about a stroke of luck." Zacchaeus laughs and then continues, "So, will you help?"

David responds, "I would like to hear Grucharse tell me why he wants to be a Teutonic knight first."

Grucharse says, "A long time before your people's colony ship arrived, evil ones came to this world. They abused the land, polluted the skies and performed unspeakable horrors on my people. It took a hundred years before we were able to drive them from this world. When your people came, we were wary of you. You do not look the same as the evil ones, but there are similarities. However, as we watched your people, we saw that you appreciated this world. You built great cities and used what the land had to offer, but you always showed respect for the natural beauty around you. We introduced ourselves to your people, not with words of course. Until Zacchaeus came along, we were not able to speak the same language, but we found ways to make our intensions known. We helped your people hunt and build their cites, and your people tended to our sick and shared your comforts with us. We like your people. Over the many years that we have cohabitated this world, some of us have even learned to understand your language; just as some of your people have learned ours. We have never before been able to speak the same language, but some of your people and mine have been able to communicate. I know much about the Teutonics and much about your Teutonic Knights.

"I also know that your colony on this planet is about to join the rest of your people in a Teutonic Union. Since the evil ones were driven from our world, we have been this world's guardians. Once this world joins your union, it will be under your protection. If you are going to protect us, it is only right that we try to help you. As Teutonic Knights, we would be able to help you protect, not just this world, but your entire union. I must confess that we like the idea of seeing other worlds and meeting more of your people.

David replies, "Well, your intentions certainly seem honorable enough, but this is not an easy decision. I need time to think it over."

Zacchaeus responds, "Yes, of course, take your time. But, if you can, I would like an answer before you leave this planet."

David leaves the laboratory. He is so torn up inside that he forgets about the banquet. David begins to aimlessly walk around, while he tries to decided what to do. He ends up back where the ship landed.

Doulphla pops her head out of the water, swims over to David, and asks him, "Can you come swim yet?"

David decides that a nice relaxing swim might help clear his head, so he accepts the invitation. He goes back into the Dove, changes into a swimming suit, comes out, and dives into the water.

Doulphla follows David as he begins to swim under the water. After about a minute, David resurfaces for air. Doulphla follows him back up.

Doulphla pops up out of the water and asks, "Why you stop swim?"

David answers, "I had to come up for air."

Doulphla replies, "Wait here."

Doulphla dives under the water and disappears from sight. After a few moments Doulphla reappears, and tosses David a strange funnel-shaped piece of coral. She says, "Use this."

David asks, "What is this, and how do I use it?"

Doulphla answers, "It's filter. Place in mouth and breath underwater. Filter stops hydrogen, but allows oxygen pass through. Try it."

David doubts that a piece of coral is going to allow him to breath under water. But he puts it in his mouth, dips his head under the water, and slowly inhales. David is surprised to discover that this filter actually works. He can breathe under water as easily as he can on dry land.

David pulls his head out of the water and tells Doulphla, "Thanks." Then the two of them begin swimming again.

Once freed from the need to resurface, David is able to dive down deep under the water. He sees incredible beauty. David sees luminescent fish and small plants of every color. David even sees a group of Dauphlines swimming in formations that start out as spheres, cubes, or pyramids, then break apart, rotate, and come back together or form flowers, trees, and beasts . The display is awesome.

Doulphla sees David's interest in the movements of the other Dauphlines. Doulphla, whose language translator can transmit speech even through water, explains that a new Dauphline has been born, and the members of the father's and mother's pods are celebrating with a dance.

David and Doulphla continue swimming for awhile. Then David notices a strange flickering light. The light is coming from a long ridge of deep pink, almost orange corals and rocks. He follows the light to one of the larger reefs. The light is emanating from a small opening that looks just big enough for a person to fit through .

David is about to enter the opening, when Doulphla swims up to him and says, "No, not enter. That bad place. Evil ones made it long ago. Must leave."

David remembers that Grucharse had said something about evil ones who came to this world a long time ago. At the time that Grucharse was telling the story, David was so engrossed with the winged wolf's abilities and their potential benefit to the Teutonics, that he didn't think much about who those evil ones were, but now David wondered just who they could have been. The only civilizations that David knew of who were capable of space travel were the Highlanders and his own people.

These evil ones don't sound anything like the Highlanders, and they certainly couldn't be Teutonics. Or could they? David knew that some of his people had allowed themselves to be corrupted. He thought about the pirates—the Buccaneers, in particular.

The Buccaneers sounded like they could have been these evil ones, but the timeline just didn't fit. This planet was colonized before the Trysham and Quanite systems. Grucharse said that the evil ones came to this planet long before the Teutonic colony ships. Then David remembers something else.

Grucharse said that there were similarities between the Teutonics and the evil ones, but that they didn't look the same. David had never thought that another species could travel through space, but this day has challenged many of David's beliefs about other species. If there is another group with space travel abilities, David decided that he had to find out all that he could about them. David swims through the opening.

Once David swims through the opening, he sees what appears to be an underwater research lab. David begins to head toward the research lab. Doulphla follows, but keeps saying that this is an evil place, and they should leave."

When David gets to the research lab, he sees an underwater entrance. He swims through the entrance and soon finds that he has entered an artificial lagoon in the midst of the research lab. He sees a computer station along one of the walls in the lagoon room. David climbs out of the water, takes the filter out of his mouth and places it in his pocket. Then David heads toward the computer station.

Doulphla pops up from beneath the water and asks, "Why you not heeded my warning?"

David responds, "Because I feel like there's something important in here. Why are you so afraid of this place?"

Doulphla answers, "Evil ones come here long time ago. They captor us, cut us open, experiment on us. They rise up to the skies and imprison winged wolves. They make sport of hunting, killing them. Poison water and many of us die. Finally, winged wolves drive evil ones from planet. We help as much as we able. Evil ones destroy much before leave."

David replies, "But if they are gone, why do you still fear this place?"

Doulphla responds, "Who know if they come back? Even if not, place maybe have traps."

David says, "If they may return, then that makes it even more important that we find out everything we can about them. You must know and understand your enemies, if you want to defeat them." David pauses momentarily and then continues, "If you want to leave, you can go. I'll be fine."

Doulphla looks scared but says, "No. I stay with you, but please make quick."

David responds, "I'll try to work as fast as I can."

Then David goes over to the computer station and activates the computer. The writing is in a language that David doesn't understand. David plugs his wrist communicator into the computer station and activates its language decipherer. After a few minutes, David's wrist communicator is able to translate the information on the computer screen. David activates his wrist communicator's data coupling subroutine and begins to download as much information from the computer's database as his wrist communicator will hold. While waiting for the download to complete, David begins searching the computer for any information on the evil ones.

David discovers that this race called itself the Technicans [Techni-cans]. These Technicans apparently believed that technology was the answer to every problem. They didn't care what they had to do to advance their technical knowledge. David also discovered that this race's most popular kind of recreation was a form of hunting wherein they would pit their advanced weapons against natural predators. He further learned that the Technicans' most elite fighting forces were a group of cyberneticly altered warriors that they called Cyber Knights.

Despite this information, David's biggest questions, "Just who are the Technicans? Where did they come from, and are they human or something else?" remained unanswered. While searching for an answer to those questions, David finds the last report recorded in the computers databank. David decides that the last report might have some clue about just where these Technicans went. David reasons that if he can find out where they went, he may be able to determine where they came from. When people are driven out of a new place, they often go back home.

The report reads, "Research Lab 302 administrator's report. Galactic standard date 14:00 02/07/39586041. The native creatures have launched a massive attack against our planetary forces. The flying wolves have destroyed all of our land stations and interstellar communications devices. It is assumed that they have also been attacking our underwater bases. This assumption is based on the fact that we have lost communication with all other research labs. We cannot confirm this assumption, because the mammal fish have apparently found a way to neutralize our underwater surveillance equipment. It appears that the native inhabitants have more intelligence than we previously believed. We have no choice but to try to get to the emergency evac point. Let's just hope that the creatures haven't found that as well. To prevent any of the other Technican companies from establishing a settlement on this planet, we are complying with company policy and activating our plague device. Long live the Kricken Company. May destruction and shame come quickly to our enemies."

After reading the planet administrator's last report, David starts to search for information on the plague device. David discovers that the plague device had two main parts—the first was the incubators, where a deadly virus was stored and bred; the second was the ejectors, where the virus was mixed with the planet's air supply and released into the atmosphere.

David is sure that this plague device is behind the Trynocn flu. When David begins to search for information on deactivating the plague devices, he trips an automated alarm system. The computer deactivates and the walls along the side of the lagoon room open to reveal about two dozen security robots. The robots begin heading for David.

David reaches for his energy blade, but it isn't there. David remembers that he left it in the Dove when he changed into his swimming suit. Quickly, he disconnects his wrist communicator from the now nonfunctioning computer station and begins to head for the lagoon. The enemy robots have him boxed in. David prays for God to hide him. As soon as the robots lose sight of David, they begin actively sealing the room. David rushes to the lagoon, but he is too late. A big metal canopy slides over the lagoon entrance. David is trapped. Although he is unable to escape, he is not in any immediate danger, because he is still invisible. David tries to figure a way out of this predicament.

Twenty minutes later, David has determined that there is no way out of the trap. He drops to his knees and begins to pray. "Father, I have searched every inch of this room and there is no way out. I cannot find anyway to reactive the computer system, and every exit is sealed tight. There is nothing that I can do to escape, but You are infinitely more capable than I. If I have found favor in Your eyes, please make a way for me to get out of this place."

As David finishes his prayer, he hears a faint crashing sound. In a few seconds, he hears a closer crash. David knows that the Lord has answered his prayer and he thanks the Lord for it. David then sees Grucharse burst through the canopy.

The robots immediately rush Grucharse, but he stands on his hind legs and uses his fore legs to bat them aside.

Then one of the robots goes over to the wall and flips a switch. The floor opens up in several places, and metal barricades with cannons mounted on them rise up from the openings. The robots take positions behind the barricades, and begin firing at Grucharse. Grucharse roars as the shots begin to hit him. Then he folds his wings in front of him, protecting his more vulnerable areas.

David leaps on top of one of the robots and rips out the wires running between its head and its body. First the robot convulses, and then falls to the floor. David grabs the cannon on top of one of the barricades and begins firing at the guns atop the other barricades.

David destroys about a quarter of the guns, before the robots know what's happening. Finally, realizing what David is doing, the robots turn all their guns against David. He ducks behind one of the barricades, while Grucharse charges the other barricades. Although the barricades are made of steel, Grucharse rips through them like they were made of plywood. David grabs one of the guns that has been torn from its barricade and rushes to the robots' rear flank. Between Grucharse's assault and David's shooting, the remaining robots are quickly defeated.

David turns to Grucharse and says, "Thank you, but how did you know that I needed help?"

Doulphla pops her head out of the water and says, "Big dome close over water, I go for help."

David says, "Well, thank you both."

Doulphla responds, "No problem. Now we leave?"

David answers, "I can't go yet. I've discovered what's causing the Trynocn flu. I think that I can find a way to stop it." David activates his wrist communicator to search through the downloaded information.

After a few minutes David exclaims, "I've found it."

Grucharse asks, "Found what?"

David answers, "One of the vice-administrator's personal logs shows that to keep anyone who didn't work for this group of Technicans from finding the plague device, the administrator had it hidden in a deep crater at the end of that corridor. The room with the crater was sealed off at he same time as the lagoon." David turns to Grucharse and continues, "Do you think that you can break down the door?"

Grucharse replies, "I don't think that will be a problem."

David and Grucharse go down the corridor and Grucharse smashes through the door. They enter the room. David notices that the crater is filled with water just as the log said. The log also said that the water was very deep.

David asks, "How long can you hold your breath?"

Grucharse answers, "A very long time."

David replies, "That is good to know, because this water is very deep."

Once David places the coral back in his mouth, he and Grucharse dive into the water. When David and Grucharse reach the plague device, David begins looking for a way to deactivate it. David discovers a flip-out panel with a keypad.

David sees that he must input the proper sequence of ten symbols into the keypad to deactivate the plague device. He once again asks God for help, and once again, the Lord answers his prayer. One by one the proper symbols seem to glow before David's eyes. Once all ten have been entered, the plague device finally deactivates. David and Grucharse head back up to the crater and get out of the water. Then they go back to the lagoon room, where Doulphla is anxiously awaiting their return.

When David and Grucharse reach the lagoon room, Doulphla asks, "How it go?"

David answers, "It went fine. We deactivated the plague device without tripping any alarms."

Doulphla hopefully asks, "Then, we go?"

David answers, "Yes, we go."

David, Grucharse and Doulphla leave the Technican base and return to the Dove. David thanks Grucharse and Doulphla for their help and promises that he will speak to Debra about letting Grucharse join the Teutonic Knights. Adino steps out of the Dove and sees David talking to Grucharse and Doulphla.

Adino says, "David, where have you been? I've been searching everywhere for you."

David thinks for a few seconds, and then replies, "Oh, I'm sorry. I forgot about the banquet, didn't I? Well, just let me change. Then I'll go back with you."

Adino responds, "No, we don't have time for that."

David asks, "Well, you don't want me to go to the banquet in my swimming suit, do you?"

Adino, who by now has become frustrated with his friend, replies, "Will you just forget about the banquet?! Ace Squadron's fighters are going into battle and you are needed right away."

David asks, "Do I, at least, have enough time to say goodbye to Sarah?"

Adino answers, "No, there's no time to get you to the hospital. In fact, the location of the battle has already been programmed into your fighter's autopilot, so you can go directly to the fighter bay. I'll tell Sarah goodbye for you."

David solemnly says, "All right." Then he hands the coral back to Doulphla and gets out of the water.

Doulphla uses her nose to bat the coral onto the ground at David's feet, and then Doulphla says, "You keep. Gift from friend."

David picks up the piece of coral, thanks Doulphla, and promises Grucharse that he'll be back to talk further about what would be the best job for Grucharse in the Teutonic Knights.

Grucharse says, "You don't have to come back. I'll go, too."

David asks, "Are you sure?"

Grucharse answers, "Yes."

Adino cuts in, "Bring him or don't bring him. I don't care, but we have to get you back to Ace Squadron station right NOW!"

David replies, "Okay, Grucharse follow me."

Adino, David and Grucharse all head for the planet's inverted gateway. After saying a very quick goodbye to Adino, David and Grucharse step through the inverted gateway and instantly arrive at Ace Squadron station.

David gets more than a few strange looks as he rushes to the hangar in his swimming suit, being followed by a huge winged wolf the people stare at even longer. Once David returns from the dog fight, he explains what happened. Soon everything goes back to normal—well, almost everything. Ace Squadron station is still the only Teutonic space station to have its very own winged wolf running around.

Chapter 8: A Trip to Brotherhood

A week after David returned to Ace Squadron station, he received a message from Brotherhood—The Teutonic capital planet. The message read, "To the Arch Duke, the stealth research team assigned to study the atmospheric gas on the planets in the Trysham and Quanite systems has just returned, and there is to be a special meeting of the House of Representatives to discuss the stealth research team's findings. Because of the unusual importance of this meeting, we request that you, rather than a proxy, be present to cast your vote. Please notify us of your estimated time of arrival at your earliest convenience."

David goes to Enoch's office and tells him, "The House is convening a special meeting, and I am going to have to personally attend. I have to request a leave of absence."

Enoch replies, "I understand. Your request is granted. However, I do hope that the House doesn't take too long to make a decision. Even though you're a first year cadet, you're one of my best pilots."

David responds, "Thank you, sir. I'll be back as soon as I can. If everything goes well at the meeting, we might just see a drop in pirate activity."

After David leaves Enoch's office, he goes to the station's long range communications room. He sends his reply to the House's message. The reply simple reads, "I got your message and will arrive tomorrow morning. The Arch Duke."

David leaves the communication room to go find Grucharse. His winged wolf companion has been housed in cargo bay five, because all of the quarters aboard the station were far too small to accommodate his massive size.

When David enters Grucharse's quarters, Grucharse says, "Hello, David, what's up?"

David answers, "I'm going to Brotherhood tomorrow, and I think that this would be a good time to talk to Debra about letting the winged wolves join the Teutonic Knights. The King has doubtless told her that it is a bad idea. But if you come and show her what an asset the winged wolves can be, I think that we have a good shot at her letting a couple of winged wolves join the Teutonic Knights—at least on a trial basis. What do you say? Are you up for a little trip?"

Grucharse answers, "I would love to see your home world. Although I do appreciate your attempt to accommodate me, this station is a little small. I would enjoy a chance to spread my wings for awhile."

David replies, "I think that you'll like Brotherhood. I've only been there once, but if my memory serves me correctly, it is quite a beautiful planet. Of course, you may not be as impressed as I was. Trynocn 7 is also a very beautiful world, and you grew up there."

Grucharse responds, "Yes. Trynocn 7 is beautiful, but remember that it is the only world that I have ever seen. Over 95 percent of Trynocn 7's surface is covered with water, and I hear that water only covers less than 60 percent of Brotherhood. I'm very excited to see a world with that much lush, green land."

David says, "Well, you'll get your chance. Right now though, I have some paperwork and packing to do. I think we should both go to sleep a little early tonight. After all, tomorrow is going to be a big day."

Grucharse replies, "You are right. Have a good night's rest, my friend."

David responds, "You, too."

David goes back to his room and begins to fill out the paperwork for his leave of absence. He packs a medium-size bag, places the bag in a corner, and takes the Duke's Blade off its shelf. The Duke's Blade is a little dusty so David cleans it, before he lays it on top of his bag. Next, David selects his best outfit from his closet. The outfit is a little wrinkled, so he irons it. Then he hangs it on a hook in front of his bed, so it will be ready for him to wear the next day. After all, this will be the first time that David will act as the Arch Duke at a House meeting and he wants to look his best. Besides, there's a chance that he might see Sarah, and for that, David definitely wants to look his best. After David is done preparing for the next day, he lays down and goes to sleep.

The next morning, David says goodbye to Josh. David meets Grucharse and they prepare to go to Crinice, the planet that

Ace Squadron station orbits. David and Grucharse will use the Crinice planet's inverted gateway to take them to Brotherhood. David and Grucharse step through the inverted gateway and step out on Brotherhood.

Grucharse says, "The reports hardly do this place justice."

Grucharse looks around him. There are large citrus vines growing around the large rocks behind him. The smell of orange blossoms permeate the air. In front of David and Grucharse are rows of blooming rosebud trees, with lilac paths running between them. To the left are several children giggling while taking turns going down a long, stone waterslide which bottoms out into a small, extremely clean pond. To the right of the duo is a large field with various kinds of fruit trees and beautiful birds flying around them.

Grucharse turns to David and asks, "Did the Great Creator craft this setting or did your people?"

David answers, "This area is the way that God made it. Other than a little weeding and trimming, we haven't touched it."

Grucharse replies, "That is what I love about your people. You don't exploit nature or even just let it alone. You nurture and take care of your land."

David responds, "Well, tending to nature has a calming and healthy effect on my people. After all, mankind was originally made to watch over a garden. I wonder if Eden looked something like this."

Grucharse asks, "Eden?"

David wistfully replies, "It was a beautiful garden—the place where the Lord God forged my people from the dust of our world.

It was our first home, before the ancestors of all humanity fell from grace and were banished for all eternity. Their descendents can never return to that place."

Grucharse wasn't sure exactly what David was talking about. Grucharse could tell that it was a story about the origin of David's people, but since Grucharse studies have not yet reached that far back in human history, he is unfamiliar with the tale.

Grucharse simply responds, "It is too bad that you were driven from your garden, but perhaps the Great Creator has looked upon your heartfelt attempts to follow Him and has given your people a new garden to live in."

David says, "Yes, perhaps He has."

David takes in a deep breath, and lets the sweet air fill his body. He lets the breath out slowly and then continues, "But I'm afraid that we can't just enjoy the scenery all day. We have to get checked into the House quarters, unpack, then find and introduce you to Debra."

Grucharse replies, "Okay, let's go."

As David and Grucharse begin to head out of the garden park, several of the children who were sliding down the stone waterslide come up to David and begin to ask him about Grucharse. "Is he your pet? What kind of an animal is he? Does he have a name? Can he do any tricks?"

David smiles and takes the time to kindly respond to each of their questions. "No, this is not my pet. He is my friend. He is a winged wolf. His name is Grucharse, and as for whether or not he can do any tricks, I think that he would like to answer that one himself."

The children are quite taken back when Grucharse responds, "Thank you, David. Yes, I can do a few tricks. Would you like to see me fly?"

One of the children, a small girl not more than six years old, answers, "Yes. Oh, please, please do fly." Grucharse spreads his wings and takes off. He flies around the children three times before landing.

The little girl says, "That was great. Do you think that I could have a ride?"

The children all shout "Yes!" and run up to Grucharse.

Grucharse looks at David and asks, "Can you check into the House quarters and unpack without me?"

David laughingly responds, "Yes, but remember that these are still children, so be careful with them."

Grucharse replies, "Don't worry. I'll be as careful as a mother with a newborn cub."

David jokingly says, "Well, you better."

David leaves Grucharse and the children and goes to the House quarters, checks in and unpacks. Once David is finished unpacking, he calls up the TKOCS, Teutonic Knight Orbital Command station. David wants to find out how soon he can speak to Debra about Grucharse.

Debra's assistant tells David, "Debra has an opening in two hours and fifteen minutes. Will you be available then?"

David answers, "Yes, that will be fine. Thank you."

Once David is finished getting an appointment with Debra, he starts trying to find out if the King, and more importantly, his daughter, have been able to return to Brotherhood yet. David discovers that the king is not expected for two more days and that Sarah is still with him on Trynocn 7. David is a little disappointed that Sarah isn't on Brotherhood yet, but he consoles himself with the fact that he should be able to see her in a couple of days.

David eats lunch and then decides to take a walk around the capital city, before his appointment with Debra. David spends about an hour walking around and admiring all the natural beauty of the Teutonic's new capital. Then he returns to the garden park where he and Grucharse parted.

When David arrives, he sees that Grucharse is still giving the children rides. David hates to interrupt their fun, but he doesn't want Grucharse to miss the appointment. So he goes to Grucharse and tells him that it is time for them meet with Debra. When the children hear that Grucharse is leaving, they are so disappointed that Grucharse, as he is leaving, promises them that he will return the next day and give them more rides.

On the way to the nearest inverted gateway, Grucharse turns to David and asks, "What do you think the chances are of Debra allowing me into the Teutonic Knights?"

David answers, "I'm not sure, but she must have accumulated a great amount of wisdom in her sixty-five years as a member of the Teutonic Knights. The other Teutonic Knights would not have elected her otherwise."

Grucharse responds, "So you think the chances are good?"

David replies, "I think the chances are fair, but you must remember that this is the first time that anyone has attempted to get a…"

David stops for a moment and thinks about the best way to phrase the rest of his statement, and then he continues, "Well, a nonhuman into the Teutonic Knights. Doubtless, she will have several questions we must answer."

Grucharse laughs, "Well then, we will just have to show Debra what a benefit winged wolves can be."

David responds, "That's what we are here for." David and Grucharse reach the inverted gateway. David sets the arrival coordinates for the TKOCS' lobby, and he and Grucharse step through the inverted gateway.

Once abroad the TKOCS, David and Grucharse head towards Debra's office. As David and Grucharse walk, Grucharse looks at all the rooms they pass. In one room, several Teutonic squires are practicing dueling with their instructors. In another room, a few scientists are testing some new kind of weapon. In the last room, the one before Debra's office, a group of Teutonic students are listening to a lecture about some of the faith-filled Teutonic Knights of the past. David and Grucharse have a few extra minutes, so they decide to stop and listen to part of the lecture, before continuing to Debra's office.

When David and Grucharse reach the doors outside Debra's office, Debra says, "Won't you come in and take a seat?" David and Grucharse enter the office. David sits in a chair directly opposite Debra, and Grucharse, being too big to fit in a chair, sits on the floor.

Debra motions with her hand toward Grucharse, and says to David, "So I take it that this is Grucharse."

David answers, "Yes."

Debra greets David and Grucharse, then turns to David and says, "Now to the matter at hand. The King has already sent me a message saying that he didn't think it was a good idea to let this, how did he put it? Oh yes, 'talking giant wolf' into the Teutonic Knights, but I know that kings can be pretty close-minded. If my memory serves me right, one of the earlier kings even opposed the first woman who wanted to join the Teutonic Knights. Petty and foolish, as far as I'm concerned, however, at other times, the kings have been right. One of the kings opposed using cloning technology to bring back our fallen knights. 'Thank God!' that we were smart enough not to engage in such an unnatural practice. I like to hear all sides of an issue before, I make a decision. Tell me why you disagree with the King."

David answers, "I am convinced that Grucharse can be a valuable addition to the Teutonic Knights."

Debra asks, "Why do you think this?"

David answers, "Grucharse is loyal, intelligent, strong, and has several special talents, like a fast healing rate and the ability to fly."

Debra replies, "He does sound like he could be useful, but there has never been a nonhuman member of the Teutonic Knights. Having one now could cause problems."

David asks, "What kind of problems?"

Debra answers, "Well, there are a couple of things right from the start—what branch of service would he be assigned to; and/or how would we know when to promote him within that branch?"

David replies, "Grucharse and I have been discussing this and think that it would be best if a new branch within the Teutonic Knights was created."

Debra asks, "What do you mean?"

David answers, "Since nonhumans don't fit well into any of the preexisting branches of service, we suggest that you create a branch specially designed for them. Like a Teutonic Knight Creature Corp."

Debra says, "It would take a lot of work to implement a new branch of service. I don't think that it would be very practical to do that for one nonhuman who wants to join."

Grucharse respectfully responds, "Excuse me, but I am not alone. There are many winged wolves who would like to join the Teutonic Knights. As you explore more planets, it is likely that more nonhumans will be found who would like to join your ranks."

Debra replies, "A Teutonic Knight Creature Corp—it is an interesting idea, but we must have each member of this Creature Corp partnered with a Teutonic Knight, to prevent…"

Debra pauses for a second while she tries to phrase her next word as diplomatically as possible, "misunderstandings." Debra turns to Grucharse and asks, "If you had to be partnered with a Teutonic Knight, would you still want to join?"

Grucharse answers, "Yes, certainly."

Debra continues, "Good."

Then she turns to David and says, "I am willing to let Grucharse join the Teutonic Knights, on a trial basis. If it works out, I will personally oversee the construction of this new Creature Corp division. Since this is your suggestion, I think it is only fair that you and Grucharse be the first set of partners. Do you both agree with these conditions?"

David and Grucharse both happily agree, and Debra says, "Good, then that's all. Dismissed."

After Debra dismisses David and Grucharse, they head for the TKOCS' inverted gateway to return to Brotherhood. Grucharse notices that David is not as happy with their success as Grucharse assumed he would be. Grucharse asks, "What's wrong? Are you unhappy with having me as a partner?"

David answers, "Of course not. I'm glad that you're in the Teutonic Knights, and I'm honored to be your partner."

David and Grucharse reach the TKOCS' inverted gateway. David programs the arrival destination. Then he and Grucharse step through.

Once David and Grucharse step onto Brotherhood, Grucharse continues, "Then what is bothering you?"

David responds, "I was just thinking about how upset the King is going to be when he discovers that I helped you get into the Teutonic Knights."

Grucharse replies, "Then do you regret helping me?"

David answers, "Not at all. I think that you will be a good addition to the Teutonic Knights, and I wouldn't take back my help, even if I could."

Grucharse, frustrated with his own lack of understanding, asks, "Then what is the problem?! From what I have read about your history, I know that you are by no means the first Arch Duke to go against the King."

David answers, "It's not going against the king that I'm sorry about. You see…"

David stops and looks around to make sure that no one is eavesdropping, and then he continues, "The Princess and I are in love. Now that I've gone against her father, he is not very likely to consent to her and I marrying."

David sighs and then says, "You probably don't understand why I'm concerned about whether or not the King approves of a marriage between his daughter and I, do you?"

Grucharse replies, "On the contrary, like Earth's red foxes, we winged wolves mate for life. I understand the stress that a difficult love can put on you. If there is anything I can do to help you and your love, please tell me."

David responds, "Thank you, but a daughter can have a tremendous influences over her parents, especially her father, and God can have even more. There is still hope for a happily ever after."

The next day, the House convenes to discuss the findings of the stealth research team that was sent to study the strange gas in the atmosphere of the planets in the Trysham and Quanite systems. After the opening prayer, the research team's chief scientist is asked to explain the team's discovery about the gas.

The chief scientist stands in the guest speaker booth, and then replies, "The gas is toxic to most nonnative plants and to all animals. However, it doesn't seem to have any effect on humans. The interesting thing about the planets in the Trysham and Quanite systems isn't the gas. It's the native vegetation."

One of the elected representatives stands and asks, "What do mean?" Then this representative sits down.

The chief scientist responds, "The native foliage possesses a previously unseen chain of nucleotides in its DNA. These nucleotides, which we have named Tryite particles, act as a super leukocyte, white blood cell, stimulant. Once introduced into the bloodstream—either through touch, injection, or digestion—these Tryite particles boost a body's natural defense system enough to fight off over 99 percent of the diseases that are currently beyond our medical technology."

Another one of the elected representatives stands and says, "These Tryite particles sound valuable, but now, the question is will the pirates be willing to trade for it?" Then this representative sits down.

Another elected representative stands and says, "The Arch Duke spent time aboard a pirate carrier." This representative turns to David and asks, "Do you think that the pirates would be willing to stop attacking our ships and begin trading with us instead?" Then this representative sits down.

David stands and responds, "We must remember that there are two major pirate factions—the Privateers and the Buccaneers. The Buccaneers have gotten rich from raiding our transport ships. I do not believe that many of them would be interested in giving up their sinful ways and taking up a lawful trade. However, the Privateers steal in order to support their families. They steal to provide the much-needed basics, like food. From my experience, I do not believe that they enjoy their lifestyle. I think that most of them would be happy to have an alternative means of keeping food on their families' tables." Then David sits and waits to see the House's response to his statements.

The King stands and says, "I am sure that the Arch Duke means well, but before the House decides to only offer a peace treaty to one of the pirate fractions, we should consider the benefits of having both factions take up lawful trade. We must remember that the Arch Duke's experience was aboard a Privateer carrier. Doubtless the information that he uncovered would be spun in favor of that faction."

David stands and says, "I apologize, if I gave the impression that I was against offering the Buccaneers the same opportunity as the Privateers. Of course, I believe that it would be better if they both took up lawful trade. However, I was asked if I thought that the pirates would be receptive to the idea. Although I think that we should offer both factions amnesty and allow them to trade with us, I believe that only the Privateer faction will agree to the offer."

Both David and the King sat down. One of the representatives prays for God's guidance. Then House began to vote on what should be done.

It does not take the House long to render an "aye" decision. A few moments after the vote, David went into the garden park outside the House quarters where he told Grucharse he would meet him after the House had made its decision. It was nearly sundown, but it didn't take David long to find Grucharse. Since the day that they had arrived on Brotherhood, Grucharse has spent nearly all his free time giving rides to the children in the garden park. So all David had to do to find Grucharse was to follow the sound of giggling children.

David meets up with Grucharse, who has just finished giving a ride. Grucharse sees David and tells the children that he is only going to give one more ride today.

David says, "You don't have to stop on my account."

Grucharse responds, "No, it's okay. I was going to stop soon anyway. The children cannot see as well as I can, so I stop giving them rides when it begins to get dark. Usually, I have already stopped by this time, but I'm giving this last ride to even out the turns."

Grucharse takes off with a child sitting on his back who is holding tight to the winged wolf's fur to keep from slipping off. This last ride takes about five minutes. When Grucharse lands, the children, knowing that the rides are finished for the day, leave for the night.

Grucharse turns to David and asks, "Well, how did it go in the House?"

David answers, "The House unanimously decided to offer the pirates a peace treaty granting them amnesty and free trade between their systems and the rest of our galaxy. Because of my experience with the Privateer faction, the House has asked me to be its emissary to the Privateers."

Grucharse replies, "Good, our first mission together."

David responds, "Yes, and let me tell you, I can sure use your help." Just then, David feels a tap on his shoulder. He turns around and sees the King.

David is about to speak, but the King begins to talk, saying, "My daughter has told me that she believes herself to be in love with you, and that you feel the same for her. Is this true?"

David is a little startled by the King's statement. David did not expect the King to already be aware of his and Sarah's feelings for each other. However David is still able to answer, "Yes, it is true."

The King replies, "I do not believe that my daughter is truly in love with you. I believe that in her youth she may be attracted to, or possibly even infatuated with you, but I believe that this will soon pass. However, because she continually protests that she is in love with you, and the Queen has implored me not to stand in the way of my daughter's happiness, I will give this so-called love a test. If you and my daughter both pass my test, I will give you my blessing. Do you think that your love can stand a test?"

David answers, "The love I feel for Sarah can withstand any test."

The King responds, "Then here it is. You and my daughter will not see, speak, or be around each other, unless forced to be by circumstances beyond the control of man, for two full years. If after that time, if you both are still willing and able to get married, I will consent. Do you understand the conditions of this test?"

David solemnly answers, "Yes." Then without speaking another word, the King leaves.

After the short conversation with the King, David feels sad that he cannot have contact with Sarah for the next two years, but he thanks the Lord for opening up a way to get the King's approval. David and Grucharse return to their quarters to pack for their return to the station. Then they use the nearest inverted gateway to return to Ace Squadron station and begin to prepare for their first official mission together.

Chapter 9: Return to the Panther

A few days have passed since David returned from his trip to Brotherhood. The House has been able to contact both pirate factions. It has asked them for a truce so that it can send its emissaries to broker a peace treaty with them.

The Buccaneers responded, "We utterly refuse any truce. We have no interest in peace. We will continue to raid whatever ships we please, and if you want to stop us, you will have to kill us."

The Privateers were more receptive and agreed to a meeting with the House's emissary. Not wanting the Buccaneers to discover the meeting until after the peace treaty is accepted or rejected, the Privateers have insisted that the meeting take place in the Bonoviane space mist. The Bonoviane mist is a nebula that blocks scanners, stealth devices, and makes weapons useless. David and Grucharse have been issued a gunboat and are currently nearing this destination.

Grucharse asks David, "Do you think that the Privateers will be likely to agree to the treaty?"

David responds, "I think that they will. We are almost to the Bonoviane space mist. Please take the ship out of Quantum flux."

Grucharse uses one of his claws to hit a few buttons on the holographic navigational panel causing the ship to exit quantum flux. Then David brings the ship into the Bonoviane space mist.

The incoming communications light turns on and David flips the two-way holographic switch. David is surprised to see a hologram of Side Blaster appear in front of his view screen.

Side Blaster also looks a bit surprised. Apparently the Privateers had no more of an idea that David was the Teutonic emissary, than David had that the Privateer carrier—where the negotiations were to take place—was the same one that he and Josh had posed as pirates.

Side Blaster mockingly says, "So you're the emissary the House sent us? I'm glad that the House sent such an honest and trustworthy Knight to broker the treaty."

David replies, "We have important business to conduct."

Side Blaster sarcastically responds, "Well then, by all means, come aboard. You do remember where docking bay three is, don't you?"

David answers, "Yeah, I remember."

Side Blaster sarcastically says, "Good, I'll roll out a red carpet for you."

Then he closes the communications line. Docking bay three's door opens, and David begins to pilot the ship inside.

While David brings their gunboat into the docking bay, Grucharse turns to him and asks, "What was all that about?"

David sighs and responds, "I once posed as a Privateer aboard this carrier in order to gain information about the pirates." David's and Grucharse gunboat enters the docking bay.

Grucharse says, "But I thought that Teutonic Knights were forbidden to lie."

Before their gunboat lands, David replies, "It's a long story. I never outright lied, but I did deceive these people, and I am not proud of it. It may have been a mistake for the House to make me their emissary."

The gunboat lands, and David steps out. He doesn't get a very warm reception. In fact, one of the Privateers pushes him back a few feet. This Privateer then raises his arm, as if to strike David. David prepares to block the blow. Then Grucharse leaps out of the gunboat, positions himself between David and the Privateer, and roars loudly at David's assailant. The man's jaw drops.

He just stands there stunned, while Grucharse says, "If any of you want to hurt my friend, you'll have to get through me first."

Just then the ship commander walks in, and yells, "What's going on here?"

Grucharse replies, "One of your men attacked the House's emissary."

The Privateer who attacked David says, "The House's emissary is one of the Teutonic Knights who posed as a pirate to betray us."

The ship commander looks at his men and says, "Regardless of what this man did, he has come here under a flag of truce and will not be harmed. Do you understand?"

The Privateers unhappily respond, "Yes, sir."

Then they began to disband. The ship commander, David, and Grucharse leave the docking bay and walk down one of the ship's corridors.

David turns to the ship commander and says, "Thank you."

The ship commander replies, "Don't thank me. Do you know how many lives we lost when you made your escape? I almost let my men lynch you."

David responds, "I regret any loss of life, but we had to get away. You were going to have us killed."

The ship commander snorts, but somehow he believes that David regrets the lives that were lost. The ship commander wonders, "If the circumstances were reversed, would I feel the same empathy for dead Teutonic pilots?" The ship commander decides that such thoughts are irrelevant. Circumstances are what they are, and they must be dealt with as such.

He continues, "Even your government considers execution to be an appropriate means of dealing with enemy spies. Do you really expect pirates to be more merciful than your own people?"

David asks, "Then why stop your people from killing me now?"

The ship commander answers, "I stopped them for two reasons. You're here under a flag of truce and to negotiate a peace treaty that might allow us to live like civilized people again."

David responds, "Oh, yes! The treaty. Are you ready to discuss it?"

The ship commander replies, "No, it's late, and it would be best to give my men time to settle down. Come, I will show you your quarters."

David asks, "What about my friend? He won't fit into any of this ship's quarters."

The ship commander answers, "Your friend can sleep in the galley. It's closed for the night and has plenty of room for him."

The ship commander turns to Grucharse and says, "I've never seen a creature like you before. If you don't mind my asking, what are you, and how did you end up here?"

Grucharse responds, "I am a Winged Wolf from Trynocn 7, and I'm here because I am David's partner."

The ship commander turns to David and says, "Oh, so that's your real name."

The ship commander, David and Grucharse arrive at David's temporary quarters. Then David turns to Grucharse and says, "Goodnight, dear friend. Thank you for coming to my aid back there. I'm sorry that I didn't thank you sooner, but I've had a lot on my mind."

Grucharse responds, "That's okay. What are friends for? Goodnight, David."

About halfway through the night, David is awakened by four men who grab him, pull him from his bed, and throw him into a holding cell.

David yells, "What's going on? The ship commander will hear about this!"

Side Blaster walks into the room where the holding cell is and says, "I don't think he'll be too likely to take your side considering that you just tried to kill him."

David exclaims, "What are you talking about!"

Side Blaster responds, "Several people, including myself, heard laser fire coming from the ship commander's office. We ran to his office and tried to get in, but the door had been jammed. Luckily, a security officer also heard the shots. He arrived and with his side arm he quickly cut the door open. When he did, I felt a man knock me down as he ran out of the office, but neither I nor anyone else could see the man. He was invisible. When I got up off the floor, I went into the commander's office. He was lying on the floor, motionless, with a laser wound in his chest. I thought he was dead, but one of the men stooped down, took the commander's pulse, and knew that the commander was still alive. We rushed the commander to the infirmary. He is currently alive, but in a coma. Since you left, I've been studying up on Teutonic Knight lore. I know some of you can turn invisible, and an invisible assailant is the only explanation for what happened to the ship commander."

David replies, "But I didn't do it. I'm here to negotiate a peace treaty, not to assassinate your commander."

Side Blaster retorts, "And why should I believe you? You've deceived us before!"

David says, "Yes, and for that I'm sorry. But if I had just tried to kill a man and knocked you down in my escape, do you really think that I would just go to my quarters and fall back to sleep? Don't you really think that I would have tried to find a way off the ship?"

Side Blaster replies, "That is the only inconsistency. That inconsistency is what is keeping you from facing the firing squad right now. Don't even think that your pet is going to come to your rescue. We've sealed the galley and placed armed guards outside it. There's no way that he's getting out alive." Then Side Blaster leaves the room.

After Side Blaster leaves, David kneels down and begins to pray, "Lord God, Jehovah, You have always been good to me. You have always given me what I need. Indeed, You have even given me the desires of my heart, and I thank you. Lord, I have been accused of a crime that I have not committed, and because of my previous deception these people won't believe what I say. What's even worse is they have imprisoned Grucharse who has never done anything to them. Please, forgive me of my sins, and help Grucharse and I to find a way out of this mess."

When David finishes his prayer, the word "infiltrator" comes into his mind. David waits for Side Blaster to come again to David's cell. He doesn't have to wait too long before Side Blaster returns.

David asks him, "Do you know what an infiltrator is?"

Side Blaster asked, "Why do you want to know?"

David replied, "When I was asking God to help me find a way to prove that I didn't commit this crime, the word infiltrator came to me. If you know what it means, please tell me."

Side Blaster answers, "You're not getting off this ship again, so I don't see what harm it can do to tell you. An infiltrator is a specially trained Buccaneer loyalty enforcer. He uses a stealth suit and various weapons to infiltrate ships which the Buccaneer counsel suspects might be planning a mutiny or not paying the proper amount of tribute. The infiltrator reports his findings to the Buccaneer counsel and tries to sabotage any dissenters activities."

David says, "Then it must have been an infiltrator who attacked the ship commander. If his stealth suit was activated, you wouldn't have been able to see him."

Side Blaster responds, "Why would any infiltrator want to attack the commander?"

David replies, "Because the Buccaneers have already refused our peace treaty. If the Privateers accept it, the Buccaneers' ally will then become their enemy."

Side Blaster says, "So they sent an infiltrator to sabotage the peace talks? I must admit that I wouldn't put it past them, but there's a flaw in your theory. We have been very careful to restrict the knowledge of where these peace talks take place and what ship would be involved. The only ones who know these particulars are people who can be trusted. How could an infiltrator have found out?"

David responds, "Maybe they didn't. This is the only ship to be infiltrated by Teutonic Knights. The Buccaneers might have thought that warranted investigation and slipped one of their infiltrators aboard when you refueled. The infiltrator could've been here for months gathering information. When I came aboard, he saw it as the perfect chance to destroy the peace talks."

Side Blaster says, "You might be right. We do have more than our share of bad luck aboard this carrier."

David responds, "Then let me go. If you've been studying Teutonic Knight lore, you should know that members of the

Teutonic Knights are trained to see in the spiritual realm as well as in the cardinal. I might be able to find him."

Side Blaster replies, "I'm afraid that I can't release you yet. There is no evidence to back up your theory. Until I find some, you are still the main suspect in this case."

David asks, "But how will you find anything, if an infiltrator can make himself invisible?"

Side Blaster answers, "He can hide his image, but a stealth suit uses a lot of energy. Now that we know what to look for, we will simply activate the ship's energy monitors. Next time he recharges, we will know right where he is. When he recharges, we can send an energy spike to the outlet he's using and fry his suit. Once he can no longer become invisible, it shouldn't be too hard for ship security to catch him."

David says, "I hope your plan works."

Side Blaster leaves the room that David is being held in. He goes to the ship's main computer room. After a couple of hours he returns.

David asks, "How did it go?"

Side Blaster responds, "Not that well."

David says, "What do you mean?"

Side Blaster answers, "Well, you were right about there being an infiltrator aboard. Ten minutes ago he used one of the outlets to recharge his suit. We sent the energy spike just like we were planning, but he must have had his suit equipped with some kind of overcharge failsafe system. When the energy spike hit his suit, he became momentarily visible. We sent station security after him, but before they could get there, he had his suit operating again. The bottom line is that he got away. Because we have no way of finding him, I have been able to convince our head of ship security to let you out. I assume you can catch him."

David replies, "I can probably apprehend him, but I don't know if I can find him in a ship this size without some help."

Side Blaster asks, "What do you have in mind?"

David answers, "Grucharse, the Winged Wolf that came aboard with me, has heightened senses, including his sense of smell. If you let him out of the galley, he can probably track this infiltrator down. Then I can capture him."

Side Blaster says, "All right, but he's probably pretty mad about being caged up. So you're responsible to make sure that he doesn't wreck the ship when we let him out. Agreed?"

David responds, "Agreed."

David and Side Blaster go to Grucharse. Grucharse begins to track the infiltrator's scent. Grucharse leads David and Side blaster through the bowels of the ship. Finally, the trio meet up with the infiltrator in the ship's construction core—the area of the ship which houses the machines which make the replacement parts for the fighters.

David sees the infiltrator and says, "Give up! I can see you. If you don't come with me voluntarily, I will have to use force!"

The infiltrator bolts. David, Side Blaster, and Grucharse pursue him. Grucharse, being faster than any human, would have been able to catch up to the infiltrator within a few seconds. But Grucharse isn't able to see the infiltrator, so he follows closely behind David. David is faster than the infiltrator and the trio gains on him.

The infiltrator runs into a large room and says, "Okay, I give up. Just don't hurt me."

Grucharse replies, "He's lying. I can smell it on him. Let David capture him."

The infiltrator says, "No, I'm telling the truth. This Teutonic Knight and his pet just want to silence me. I saw the knight try to murder your commander."

Side Blaster says, "If you saw him, then why didn't you report what you saw to station security?"

The infiltrator says, "Because you had already captured him, and I didn't want to blow my cover, if it wasn't necessary."

David raises his voice and says, "He's lying. You've got to believe me."

The infiltrator says, "No, the knight is the one who's lying, just like before."

Side Blaster says to the infiltrator, "If you want me to believe you, then deactivate your stealth suit and put your hands in the air. Then wait right there without moving, while I come to arrest you. I'll make sure that David and his wolf don't touch you."

The infiltrator says, "Sure, whatever you say. Just keep them away from me." Then he deactivates his stealth suit and raises his hands.

Side Blaster begins to walk toward the infiltrator, but David grabs Side Blaster's shoulder and says, "Don't do it. It's a trap."

Side Blaster replies, "I'll be on my guard."

Side Blaster walks toward the infiltrator. When Side Blaster gets about ten feet away, the infiltrator quickly jumps up and pulls a handle located approximately two and a half feet above his head. A crane holding construction supplies above Side Blaster's head opens. David dives and tries to push Side Blaster out of the way, but doesn't completely make it. One of the metal girders lands on Side Blaster's leg pinning him down and causing him to grimace in pain.

Side Blaster screams as the girder continues to crush his leg. Grucharse rushes to help, but the rest of the supplies fall across the corridor's opening and Grucharse is too large to make it through. David, who had slid past the falling equipment, draws the Duke's Blade. He tries to cut the girder and free Side Blaster, but just as David reaches the girder, the infiltrator tackles him. The Duke's Blade goes flying out of David's hand. David kicks the infiltrator off of him. David runs for his blade, but the infiltrator being closer to the blade, gets it first.

The infiltrator says to David, "Now, Teutonic Knight, you will die by your own weapon."

David says, "The Lord will strengthen me to defeat you." Then David grabs his laser disk, activates it, and prepares to do battle.

The infiltrator says, "We'll see." Then he rushes David.

David sidesteps the infiltrator, but then the infiltrator turns and tries to cut David from the shoulder to the ribs. David uses his laser disk to deflect the blow, and then David slices at the infiltrator's belly. The infiltrator jumps back to avoid David's slice, but he still gets a little cut. The infiltrator tries to bring the energy blade down on David's head. David brings up his laser disk and blocks the blow. The infiltrator continues pushing down, and David, fighting both the infiltrator and gravity, begins to lose ground. The infiltrator laughs as the energy blade gets closer and closer to David's skull.

When David realizes that he can't hold out much longer, he throws his weight onto his right leg and uses his left leg to kick the infiltrator as hard as he can in the gut.

The infiltrator falls back, but so does David. David gets up just in time to see the infiltrator running at him, while swinging the energy blade from side to side.

While backing away from to the charging infiltrator, David blocks the infiltrator's swings. The infiltrator swings right, then left, then right, then left, then left, then right three times, and then down. David continues to deflect each of the infiltrator's blows as he backs up.

Then the infiltrator thrusts at David. David sees his opening. He turns sideways avoiding the infiltrator's thrust, and then David cuts the tip of the Duke's Blade's handle off. The Duke's Blade makes a TSCHU sound as it short circuits and deactivates.

The infiltrator begs David to spare his life. David agrees. Then he reaches into one of the compartments on his belt, pulls out a neural disrupter, and puts it on the nape of the infiltrator's neck. David goes back to where he left Side Blaster and uses his laser disk to cut Side Blaster free.

Then David asks him, "Are you okay?"

Side Blaster responds, "Nothing the ship's medic can't fix. What happened to the infiltrator?"

David replies, "With God's help, I caught him. He is over there."

Side Blaster says, "You made sure that you tied him up as tight as possible, right? Infiltrator's are trained to escape from just about anything."

David says, "I doubt he'll escape. I put a neural disrupter on the nape of his neck. He will be paralyzed from the neck down until its removed."

David helps Side Blaster hobble over to the infiltrator. Side Blaster takes a pair of convict bracelets out of his belt and limping behind the infiltrator places them on the infiltrator's wrist and removes the neural disrupter. In the meantime, David picks up the two pieces of his Duke's Blade to assesses the damage. He decides that the damage isn't too bad. The cut is smooth. It shouldn't take more than a couple of hours in a machine shop to repair it, which is a good thing, too. David hates to think that in less than six months, he could have managed to destroy a blade that has lasted for hundreds of years.

David and Side Blaster bring the infiltrator to the corridor were Grucharse is. There is just enough room for the humans to squeeze by the construction material. David goes first, then the infiltrator, followed by a limping Side Blaster. Grucharse growls at the infiltrator as he passes.

With the infiltrator in custody, David is set free. A few days later, the commander is feeling better. The peace talks begin, and it doesn't take long for David to convince the Privateers to agree to the treaty. Having caught the man who tried to kill the ship commander and having provided a lawful way for the Privateers to support their families, David and Grucharse depart the Panther on good terms.

Chapter 10: Into the Labyrinth

It has been a few weeks since David and Grucharse brokered the peace treaty with the Privateers. The number of pirate raids had dropped off considerably allowing David and Grucharse to take more ground missions. Even though the ground missions had increased, since David was assigned to Ace Squadron station, he still has special patrol missions and some escort missions. The fighter crafts used for the flying missions are streamlined and require skill and dexterity to pilot. Because Grucharse is unable to pilot a fighter, or even fit into one, he is forced to remain aboard the station, when David is assigned special missions requiring the fighter's use. But since David hasn't seen much combat on these missions lately, Grucharse doesn't feel like he's missing out on too much. David and Grucharse, having been summoned to receive their latest mission, head to Enoch's office.

On the way to Enoch's office, Grucharse turns to David and asks, "When you received the message summoning us to Enoch's office, did the message say anything about what kind of mission we were going to be sent on?"

David replies, "No, but it must be a ground mission, if they want both of us at the briefing."

Grucharse responds, "I hope so. The corridors on this station are a little small for my tastes. I'm looking forward to getting another chance to spread my wings."

David says, "Yeah, I'm sorry. I'm afraid that this station wasn't exactly designed to accommodate anyone the size of a winged wolf."

Grucharse replies, "It's not too bad, and it's worth it. At least I can stretch out in my cargo hold. A slight bit of discomfort is a small price to pay for the honor of being the first of my kind to join the Teutonic Knights. I again thank you for that."

David responds, "You don't have to thank me. You are a welcomed addition, and I hope that more of your race will be able to join us."

Grucharse says, "I'm sure they will, now that they're allowed to. Before I left Trynocn 7, many of my pack expressed their desire to work with your champions of justice."

David and Grucharse reach Enoch's office and enter. Enoch has a bit of a grim look on his face as he says, "Your new mission is a dangerous one. In fact, we've already lost two knights where we're sending you."

David replies, "God rest their souls and take them unto Him."

Enoch responds, "We're not sure that they're dead."

David asks, "What do you mean?"

Enoch replies, "We lost contact with the knights two days ago. They were alive when we lost contact, but they were in a very dangerous area and could be dead by now. Whether or not they are still alive is one of the things we want you to find out."

David responds, "So this is a rescue mission?"

Enoch answers, "No. That is only part of it. If the two knights are still alive, finding them is top priority. But this is an intelligence gathering mission.

"Ever since you returned from Trynocn 7, we have been studying the information that you were able to download from the Technican database and trying to learn everything we could about this seemingly dangerous race. We even sent out unmanned space probes to scan for energy signals similar to what your wrist communicator recorded in the Technican base. Last week, one of our probes found a matching energy signal on a planet in the Charock system. We used one of our inverted gateways to send two knights to investigate."

David says, "I take it that those are the two knights you've lost contact with."

Enoch replies, "Yes. One of the knights is still a student, but she is very intelligent. She was selected for this mission, because during her student studies, she took part in the project to decode and retrieve the password protected information that you downloaded into your wrist communicator. Although she was only supposed to be an assistant in the project, she is gifted with computers. She is largely responsible for the information that we have been able to decode. The other knight on the mission team has reached the rank of Elite Teutonic Knight. He was chosen for this mission because he excels at combat, has great faith, and has much experience in avoiding enemy traps."

David asks, "Traps?"

Enoch responds, "Yes. Our scans indicated that the energy signatures emanate from somewhere within a large underground maze. We can use the inverted gateway to send you into the maze. But something in the maze prevents us from pinpointing the exact source of the energy readings, so you will have to navigate the maze to find the source of the readings. Not only do you have to find the other two knights, and navigate the maze while avoiding all the traps; you will also have to discover a way to shut down the dampening field that surrounds the planet."

David asks, "What kind of dampening field?"

Enoch answers, "A level nine energy dampening field. The dampening field prevents energy from flowing in a complete circuit. The maze itself is protected from the dampening effect, but the field surrounds the planet and prevents us from being able to safely pick you up after the mission. Consequently, no electrical devices will work outside of the maze. I don't much like the idea of sending you two into this maze without backup or a way to pull you out, if things turn sour. In fact, I tried to convince my superiors to send a squad of knights with you. But after losing the two knight team that had been trained for this mission, my superiors decided that this mission was too dangerous to send a full squad. They decided that the most effective knights for this mission would be the two who successfully infiltrated the Technican base on Trynocn 7."

David says, "I understand. When do we leave?"

Enoch replies, "As soon as you're ready. We already have an Avenger class ship in the Charock system waiting to pick you up once you've deactivated the dampening field."

Enoch hands David a data pad and continues, "Here are the inverted gateway arrival coordinates. Once you have all the equipment that you need, head down to Crinice (the planet that Ace Squadron station orbits) input the coordinates, and begin your mission. Don't forget to bring a solar communicator so you can contact the ship that is assigned to retrieve you. If you have to speak to anyone else, the ship is fitted with a long-range communications device and can relay your messages to virtually any of our planets."

David responds, "I'll remember."

David and Grucharse gather the equipment that they think might be useful for the mission and then take a passage shuttle down to mission Crinice. Once they reached Crinice's inverted gateway, David input the coordinates. Then David and Grucharse stepped into the Technican maze.

The walls of the maze have so much dirt and sand on them that no matter where David looks, he cannot see the metal underneath. Many sections of the walls are also covered by vines. There is a small amount of yellow light emanating from the fluorescent tubes that run through the ceiling. Due to the filth on the tubs and the maze's obvious power shortage, it is difficult for David to see more than thirty feet in front of him. David pulls his equipment pack off his back, opens it and pulls out two SEVs—Sight Enhancing Visors—an energy tracer and the solar communicator. He offers Grucharse a SEV, but Grucharse says that he can see fine. David puts one of the sight enhancing visors back into the equipment pack, closes up the pack and puts it back on his back. Then David puts the visor on his head and activates it.

David activates his solar communicator, so that he can let the retrieval ship know that he is within the Technican maze. However, when he tries to establish contact with the retrieval ship, all he gets is static. He tries again to contact the retrieval ship and again only static responds.

David says, "Well, I guess this explains why we lost contact with the other two knights. Something down here must be capable of jamming a solar communicator."

Grucharse replies, "I didn't know it was possible to jam a solar communicator."

David responds, "Any communicator can be jammed. We have never before encountered a race, other than our own, that had the technology to do it."

Grucharse asks, "Is it possible that the communicator could be malfunctioning or that something could be wrong aboard the retrieval ship?"

David answers, "Anything's possible, but that is unlikely. I checked the communicator before we left, and if something had gone wrong aboard the retrieval ship, Enoch would have told us during the briefing."

Grucharse says, "This does not bode well. If their technology is advanced enough to jam a solar communicator, who knows what else it can do."

David replies, "That's what we're here to find out."

Grucharse responds, "The history of the Technicans dwelling on our world has been passed down through generations. I cannot stand thinking of the atrocities they committed, their horrible experiments, their hunting us down simply for fun, and how we barely were able to drive them from our planet!"

David can tell that Grucharse is getting agitated, so David interjects and tries to calm down his friend. David says, "It's okay. That happened a long time ago. The Technicans are gone from your planet. Judging by the condition of this place, I doubt that any of them have been through here in a long time."

Grucharse responds, "You're right. I just fear for my race, if the Technicans were ever to return. Whenever I thought about the Technicans, I have always taken comfort in the knowledge that your people are very advanced and would doubtless come to our aid. But if the Technicans have grown as advanced or possibly even more advanced than you, my comfort is gone. I cringe when I think of them committing the same atrocities again."

David replies, "So far all we know is that the Technican's are about as advanced as us in the field of stellar communications. That doesn't mean that they are necessarily as advanced in other fields. And even if they are, Jehovah is on our side and He is infinitely more powerful than anyone or anything could ever be."

Grucharse calmly says, "Thank you. I feel better now. Please forgive me for my previous outburst."

David replies, "Don't worry about it."

Grucharse responds, "Then let's get back to the mission. Is your energy tracer picking up anything?"

David answers, "Yes. There is an energy pattern matching that of a Technican database coming from that passageway."

Grucharse says, "Then let's get going."

They head down the passageway. After walking no more than forty feet, two large blast doors, one in front of them and the other behind them, lower and seal them in. Then the floor beneath them begins to separate revealing a deep chasm. Luckily the passageway is large enough for Grucharse to spread his wings. Grucharse grabs David and hovers above the chasm. Grucharse flies to the blast door in front of them. Once there, David grabs his Duke's Blade and begins cutting through the door. Before he can finish cutting through, the blast doors open and the floor comes back together automatically. Grucharse puts David down, and then lands.

David says, "I take it that that was one of the traps Enoch told us about."

Grucharse replies, "I'd say so, but how did we activate it?"

David responds, "I think I know."

David reaches up and pushes some of the buttons on the side of his SEV. David continues, "Just as I thought. There are a number of infrared beams crossing the floor. We must have broken one and that triggered the trap. The trap must have a time-delayed reset that returns the passageway to normal after the one caught inside would have plummeted to his death. I'll keep my SEV set to scan the infrared spectrum from now on. Hopefully, we can avoid anymore of those traps."

David takes off his equipment pack, pulls out the other SEV and says, "I think that you should use the other SEV so that you can see the infrared beams, too."

Grucharse replies, "I agree." David puts the SEV on Grucharse's head and programs it to scan the infrared spectrum. They continue down the passageway until it forks into two smaller passageways.

Grucharse asks, "Which way?"

David replies, "The tracer is picking up stronger energy signatures from the right side passageway."

Grucharse says, "All right, we go right." David and Grucharse head down the right passageway, but it begins narrowing.

Soon the passageway becomes so small that Grucharse is forced to tell David, "I'm sorry, but I can't continue any further down this passageway. I'll head back to where the first passageway split into two and try taking the left passage. Maybe that one will not become as small as this one has."

David replies, "Okay, but be careful. Take one of these signaling devices and I'll keep the other. This way we can find each other if one of us gets lost. Remember that this is a deadly maze. We have already encountered one trap, but there are doubtless more."

Grucharse responds, "I'll be careful."

David says, " May God watch over you."

Grucharse replies, "And you, too." Then they separate.

As David continues down the passageway it continues to shrink. David ends up having to clip his energy tracer to his belt and crawl through the last thirty feet of the passageway. Finally, David reaches its end. It ends in a small room with one door directly opposite the entrance from the passageway. David enters the small room and as he does, all of the energy is sucked from his SEV's power unit. He takes the SEV off his head and thinks to himself, "There must by an energy leech field in this small room." David notices that he can still hear his energy tracer beeping. The energy leech field can't be more than a level two, because the insulation around the energy tracer's power unit is keeping it from being drained. Although the room is small, it is large enough for David to stand up and move around. He grabs his energy tracer and scans the room. The energy signal is coming from beyond the door. He feels a peculiar uneasiness as he opens the door. David decides that this time he will look before he leaps. Beyond the door, he see a relatively large, dark room that is only illuminated by three faint beams of light—one red, one blue and one green—located in the center of the room. The poor illumination makes it difficult for David to determine what awaits him inside, but knowing that he must continue in his mission, David walks through the doorway. The split second after he walks through the doorway, the door slams shut behind him and an energy field covers the door and the walls.

The slamming of the door awakens two people who had been sleeping in the room. The two people quickly grab their energy blades and activate them. David tries to calm the two.

David says, "Wait, put down your weapons. I'm a Teutonic Knight. My name's David, and I'm not going to hurt you."

One of the knights responds, "David? As in the Arch Duke David?"

David replies, "Yes."

The knight says, "Oh, David, it is good to see you again!"

David says, "Zipporah?"

Zipporah answers, "Yes! What are you doing here?"

David responds, "The House sent me here to find you two and help you complete your mission." Zipporah frowns.

David asks, "What's wrong?"

Zipporah answers, "I'm glad to see you, but I wish you hadn't come. I know that the House was trying to do the right thing by sending someone in to find us, but now you're trapped along with us."

The other knight says, "Come on, Zipporah. God will get us out of this."

Zipporah replies, "Yes. Moseus, I know that you're right. I just have to keep having faith, focusing my eyes on God, and not on our predicament. I do believe that God will deliver us, according to His will and timing."

David asks, "What do you mean by trapped and predicament?"

Moseus responds, "This room is a trap, and the only way to get out is to solve the riddle of the room."

David asks, "What's this riddle?"

Moseus and Zipporah bring David to the left wall of the room. David notices that there are markings on the wall. The markings are similar to what David had seen in the Technican's underwater base on Trynocn 7, but there are enough discrepancies to make it difficult for David to read them. David is about to ask for God's help, but Zipporah begins to read the markings aloud.

She reads, "With none, you are blind. With a little, you can see. With a lot, you are blind again."

David looks at Zipporah and asks, "Where did you learn to read these markings?"

Zipporah answers, "I spent a long time studying the information you brought back from the Technican base. In it there were listings of over thirty different Technican tribes, each with their own dialect of the Technican root language. I memorized all of the variations before Moseus and I began this mission."

David says, "That must have taken a long time."

Zipporah responds, "Not that long, about a month."

David replies, "That's a dialect a day. I'm impressed. God must have given you a real gift for languages."

Moseus says, "That's what I told her when she first read the riddle to me."

David is so impressed by Zipporah's knowledge of the Technican language that he momentarily forgets the task before them. Then David remembers about the riddle, thinks for a moment and then says, "Light! The answer must be light."

Moseus replies, "That is the same answer that Zipporah and I came up with, but light is not one of the choices on the answer wall."

David says, "The answer wall?" Then Zipporah and Moseus bring David to the wall opposite the one with the riddle. Once David is close enough to the wall, he sees that this wall also bears Technican markings.

Zipporah starts to read them aloud, "Those who seek the mighty power of the knowledge of science and its almighty child technology must first prove their worth by choosing the correct answer to the riddle of the room. Those who lack the intelligence to solve the riddle are unworthy and are doomed to starvation. Your choices are eyes, ears, stars, moons, darkness, blue, red, green, yellow, cyan, magenta, heat, optical enhancers, wisdom, life, and death."

Once Zipporah is finished reading aloud, Moseus says, "We have tried many things to get out of here. The last thing we tried was using some of the reflective objects that are scattered around the walls of this room to reflect the red, the green, and the blue beams of light to their respective color names on the answer wall."

Zipporah says, "The color names must have spectral scanners in them, because as each light color was positioned over its name, we heard a click from the exit door. We thought that we were finally going to be able to get out of here. But after we had finished redirecting the light, the door still didn't open.. We returned things to the way they were, until we could think of something else to try."

David says, "Well, if the exit door was clicking, it would seem that you were on the right track."

David thinks for a moment and then asks, "You said that the answer wall had yellow, cyan and magenta in addition to red, blue and green, right?"

Zipporah replies, "Yes. Why?"

David says, "Red, green and blue light are the three primary light colors, and if you mix them in different amounts you can make the human eye see any known color. If we use the reflective objects, we should be able to combine the colors to form a yellow, cyan and magenta beam of light."

Zipporah responds, "But when you mix the three primary colors of light to form one of the other light colors, the new color doesn't actually posses the same wavelength that corresponds to the true color of that light. You can fool the human eye, but I doubt that it would work on the sensor housed in the name of that color on the answer wall."

David replies, "Under normal circumstances, I would agree with you. But this room is one giant riddle. When someone creates a riddle, they usually design it so that it can be solved. Given the Technican's assumed level of technological development, they could have easily designed spectral sensors to interpret light the same way as a human eye. Besides what do we have to lose if we try?"

Zipporah says, "You've got a point. Moseus, what do you think?"

Moseus responds, "Well, we've tried everything else that we could think of."

The three of them begin working on David's plan. After about ten minutes, they have successfully used the red, blue and green lights to form first yellow, then cyan, and finally magenta. As each new light beam was formed, it was directed towards its respective name. As each light reached its name, the exit door clicked, but the door didn't open. The three Teutonic Knights set to work disassembling the new color so that they could mix the primary red, blue and green lights to form another one of the three other colors listed on the answer wall. After they finished trying the yellow light, the cyan light, and the magenta light, they tried to think of what else they could do to escape the room in which they were trapped.

David says, "The door clicked each time we directed a light color to its name, but the door didn't open. Maybe we need to have all the light beams on their respective names at the same time."

Moseus replies, "I hope not. We only have three beams to work with and six names. We would only have half of what we need, and that's without considering the fact that in order to get the yellow, cyan, and magenta we have to use combinations of the three primary light colors. We don't have enough beams to activate all the spectral sensors at once."

Zipporah responds, "I think we do."

David asks, "How?"

Zipporah answers, "There are a lot of reflective objects that we still haven't used. If we position some of the extras properly, we can…"

David joins Zipporah in her answer, "Split the three beams that we have into nine."

Moseus says, "And with the nine beams, we can direct one of the red beams to the red answer, one of the blue beams to the blue answer and one of the green beams to the green answer. And then, we can combine the remaining six beams of light to form yellow, cyan and magenta and direct them to those answers."

They all execute their new plan. As each beam of light strikes its respective names, the exit door clicks, and when all the beams of light are on their respective names, at last the exit and entrance doors both open. After saying a prayer of thanks to God, the three knights finally leave the room that they have been trapped in and enter a large room with two computers in it.

Zipporah goes to one of the computers and says, "This looks like the computer responsible for regulating all of the labyrinth's traps and defenses. I should be able to shut down the dampening field and communications jamming device from here."

Moseus goes over to the other computer and adds, "This looks like an encyclopedia database. When I hook up the data decryption computer we brought with us, we can start downloading the files. Once we've finished, we'll have at least ten times more information about the Technicans."

David responds, "Okay, I'll go and radio for pickup. When you two are done, meet me at the large end of the shrinking passageway. You do know which one that is, don't you?"

Zipporah nods her head in agreement, and then she asks, "Where are you going?"

David replies, "I've got to get my partner."

Moseus says, "Okay, we should be there in about fifteen minutes."

David leaves Zipporah and Moseus and heads back to where he and Grucharse separated. Then he begins to look for his friend. He takes his signaling device out of his equipment pack, but soon discovers the energy leech field drained the signaling device's power unit. Luckily, Grucharse's signaling device is still operating and David is able to use his energy tracer to track his friend. David finds Grucharse quickly.

When Grucharse sees David, Grucharse asks, "How did you do? Did you find the two lost knights or the information that we were seeking?"

David responds, "Yes, I found the other two knights and together we were able to gain access to a Technican data repository. We were also able to shut down the dampening field that surrounds this planet. As soon as we meet up with the other two knights, Zipporah and Moseus, we can radio for pickup and get off this planet."

Grucharse replies, "That's good. The sooner we get out of here the better."

David asks, "What are you holding?"

Grucharse answers, "Oh. In the wake of your good news, I almost forgot to tell you. While I was trying to find a way around that *shrinking passageway*, I entered a room that had another trap. As soon as I stepped within the room, all the exits sealed and the room quickly flooded with toxic gases. Because my species has an inborn resistance to most toxins and poisons, I was able to survive long enough to smash a hole through one of the sealed doors in the room and allow the toxic gasses to escape. Once I was out of danger, I noticed that there were some old Technican cybernetic limbs and implants in the corner of the room. They must have come from a Technican Cyber Knight who became trapped within that room and was unable to survive the toxic gas. It must have happened a long time ago, because all that was left were his cybernetic parts. Anyway, I thought that if your scientists had some of the Technican Cyber Knight parts to study, it might help. I grabbed the parts before I finished smashing down the door and escaped the room."

David responds, "Yes, I'm sure that our scientists will find implants from one of the Technican's elite soldiers quite useful. Good job, Grucharse."

David puts the parts into his equipment pack, and then continues, "Come on, Moseus and Zipporah said that they would meet us at the entrance to the shrinking passageway in fifteen minutes, and it's rude to be late."

David and Grucharse head to their rendezvous with Zipporah and Moseus. The other two knights are already waiting, when David and Grucharse arrive. David radios for pickup and before long, the four knights have left the Technican planet behind them.

Chapter 11: A New Assignment

Weeks have passed since David's and Grucharse's return from the Technican Labyrinth. Since then, ground assignments have become scarcer and the Privateer treaty has brought much peace. Consequently, David hasn't had much to keep him occupied these last few weeks. He finds his thoughts turning more and more to Sarah. However, he knows that he can't have any communication with her for nearly two years. The more he thinks about her, the more he longs for her and the sadder he becomes. So when Enoch calls David to his office to discuss a new assignment, David is quite excited about the aspect of getting his mind off of Sarah and onto a mission.

David walks into Enoch's office and says, "Sir, I heard that you wanted to see me about a mission."

Enoch says, "Not a mission, an entirely new assignment."

David asks, "What do you mean by an entirely new assignment?"

Enoch responds, "Earlier today, Joseph, who is the head of the Conscripter division of the Teutonic Knights, contacted me. He said that the House is impressed with the job you did negotiating the Privateer treaty, especially under the circumstances, and they suggested that you would make a good Conscripter."

David says, "I've never heard of a Conscripter before."

Enoch says, "I'm not surprised that you haven't heard of them. They are a relatively new division. They were created shortly after we left earth."

David asks, "So what does a Conscripter do?"

Enoch answers, "As you are well aware, we have been sending colony ships into outer space for the last 150 years. A Conscripter goes to these colonies and invites them to join the Teutonic Union."

David thinks about the offer. The position does sound exciting and would keep him active. It would help him get his mind off Sarah. But David doesn't want to leave his friends.

David says, "It sounds like an interesting occupation, but it means leaving all of my friends. Besides, I don't know anything about conscripting."

Enoch responds, "Don't worry about that. A new Conscripter is always paired with an experienced team on the first mission. The team will teach you everything you need to know. Also, you won't have to leave all of your friends. Grucharse, being assigned as your partner, will be transferred with you."

David replies, "I don't know, sir. What do you think? Would you accept the transfer?"

Enoch answers, "No, I wouldn't. I've been a member of the space force far too long to be anything else. But if I were like you, a new pilot just starting his tour of duty, I think that I would. You are one of my best pilots, but I can tell that over the last few weeks you've been getting restless. These are relatively peaceful times, and I'm grateful for the sake of the Teutonic citizenship. But flying endless escort missions and rotten patrols is no life for an Ace Squadron pilot. A fighter pilot is not like a civilian pilot. He's a soldier—a war-bird. He needs a good dog fight every once in awhile, or he loses his sense of accomplishment and falls into a rut. I'm sure that everyone on the station will miss you. Honestly, I don't think that there are many of them who wouldn't trade places with you, if they had the chance. Since the Privateer treaty went into effect, there really hasn't been much work for fighter pilots. We should try to start reassigning some of them anyway."

David says, "Well, I would like to talk to Grucharse. If he will be coming with me, he should be consulted."

Enoch replies, "Of course. I can't imagine the winged wolf turning down a transfer that gets him more ground time, but you're right. You should discuss it with him. Joseph isn't contacting me again until tomorrow. Go and talk to Grucharse. Then come to me and tell me what you've decided."

David leaves Enoch's office and goes to repair bay five, which is Grucharse's quarters. As David enters the repair bay, He hears Grucharse say, "Hi, David, what did Enoch want to see you about?"

David replies, "He wanted to know if we were interested in a transfer."

Grucharse says, "A transfer, to what?"

David answers, "To the Conscripters, a group of Teutonic Knights that go to the various colonies and offer them admittance into the Union."

Grucharse, a little worried that David's transfer could mean their separation, asks, "What did you say?"

David responds, "I told him that since you are my partner and would be transferring with me, I would have to see how you felt about it."

Grucharse, no longer worried about losing his partner, replies, "I think that it sounds like a dangerous and risky assignment."

Grucharse pauses for a moment before continuing, "I say we take it, before someone else does."

David says, "I had no idea that you were such an adventure seeker."

Grucharse responds, "Are you kidding? I love being a Teutonic Knight, and I'm happy to be your partner. But I'm less than thrilled with our current assignment. There's not much that I can do aboard a fighter station. I can't even fit into the fighters. All I do is wait around for you to pull another ground mission. To be perfectly honest, I'm a little worried that my service record isn't going to be impressive enough for Debra to form the Creature Corp, and the rest of my pack will never be able to join at all."

David replies, "Don't worry about that. I'm sure that your service record is plenty impressive. You've only been a knight for a few months. Most knights would still be in training. You've already been invaluable on the only missions that got Teutonics information about the Technicans. And you helped broker an important peace treaty. Still, I do see your point about wanting to get out more. To tell the truth, I've felt a little boxed in myself. I'll tell Enoch that we'll take the job."

The next day, David tells Enoch that he has talked to Grucharse and they have decided to take the job. Enoch replies, "Good, I'll tell Joseph when he calls." Then David leaves to go on a patrol mission along with Josh and Esther.

While on patrol, Esther says, "I hate patrol missions. They're so boring. Your autopilot flies your fighter in a prearranged pattern while your sensors automatically scan for anything out of the ordinary. If the scanner actually finds anything, your fighter just beeps so that you can make a record of what caused the beep. Remind me again why we don't just let the autopilot do this job by itself. There has got to be something more important for us to do than baby-sit a fighter."

Esther always complained about patrol missions. Of course, she did grow up as a pirate, and David doubted that the pirate pilots had to fly very many patrol missions. Esther's been at Ace Squadron station for over six months now. David would have thought that she would be used to patrol missions by now. David remembered that when Esther, Josh and he had fled from the pirates, she had made David promise that he would make her a Teutonic pilot in exchange for her help. David agreed, but only if she was able to pass all the exams that a normal cadet would. David had planned to use his authority as Arch Duke to get Esther transferred to Ace Squadron station when her training was finished. As it turned out, he didn't need to use his authority. Esther finished the training at the top of her class and got assigned to Ace Squadron station completely on her own merits. She was a fine pilot. Although David never would have believed it when they first met, he was happy to call her a friend.

David is brought back to the present when he hears Josh reply, "I'm with Esther on this one. The brass say that they want us here, because if the ship encounters an enemy, it needs its pilot. But in the year that I've been a member of Ace Squadron, I've flown over fifty patrol missions and have yet to encounter an enemy on any of them."

David responds, "You two are always complaining about patrol missions. Why don't you just try to concentrate on something else? You'll find the time goes by much faster."

Josh says, "Okay. So David, are you going to take that new Conscripter job?"

David responds, "How do you know about that job?"

Josh says, "Esther told me."

David asks Esther, "And how did you find out?" Esther is quiet, but in his display, David can see her lip curling into a small smile.

David continues, "Oh, no! Please tell me that you didn't bug Enoch's office."

Esther replies, "NO! I just happened to be using my room communicator when Joseph called, and by some fluke my equipment picked up the message."

David responds, "It must have been some fluke considering that the personal communicators in our rooms and the station's secured communication systems are on completely different circuits!"

Esther laughs lightly and says, "Okay, okay, I tapped my room's communicator into the secured com system, but I was telling the truth when I said that I haven't bugged Enoch's office."

David responds, "Esther, Esther, Esther, when are you going to learn to trust your squadron and your leaders?"

Esther makes an insincere pout and replies, "Sorry. I guess once a pirate, always a pirate." Then she laughs again.

Josh pipes in, "I think that we have gotten a little off track. David, you still haven't answered my question. Are you going to take the transfer?"

David replies, "Yes, I'm sorry that I didn't tell you. I was going to wait for a good opportunity."

Josh says, "Don't worry about it. Although I will miss you, I've known for awhile that it was only a matter of time before you got transferred to another division."

David asks, "How?"

Josh says, "Well, to start with, it was never your dream to be a pilot. When we were kids, while I was pretending to fly through asteroid fields and shoot down enemy space crafts, you were always pretending to have energy blade fights and to escape from imaginary traps. When Grucharse became your partner, it didn't make much sense for you to be assigned to a division where he couldn't go on most of your missions."

Josh hears a beeping sound. He looks at his display panel and sees that the autopilot is already inputting the fighters' return path into the navigational computer and is prompting the pilot to authorize the shift into Quantum flux. He says, "Already? That was fast."

David replies, "See, I told you that if you have to do something boring, you should just occupy your mind with something else. The time will go by much faster."

Esther pipes in and says, "Well, come on, let's get back to the station, unless you boys enjoy flying around the middle of nowhere."

Josh laughs and answers, "Not in the least." Then David, Josh and Esther head for home.

When David gets back to the station, the bot assigned to download the patrol mission's logs tells him, "Sir, Enoch would like to see you at your earliest convenience."

David says, "Thank you," and heads to Enoch's office.

When David gets to Enoch's office, Enoch says, "Well, you should consider yourself lucky. Your transfer went through, and Elijah has requested that you and Grucharse be partnered with him and John for the first of your new assignments. We have been having some problems with the inverted gateway on the planet below us. So instead of you using that gateway to get aboard Elijah's ship, he is coming to the station. He'll be here in a couple of days to pick you and Grucharse up."

A few days later, Elijah's ship, the Olive Branch, docks at the station. Nearly everyone on the station is in the docking bay waiting to greet their guests. Most of the Teutonic pilots are eager to meet Elijah, whose faith is legendary, but David and Josh are more excited about seeing John again.

As soon as the Elijah steps off the Olive Branch, David and Josh can feel the Spirit of God fill the docking bay. Then Enoch walks to Elijah and says, "Elijah, my old friend, it is good to see you again."

Elijah replies, "Thank you. It is good to see you also. How long has it been?"

Enoch responds, "Just this side of ten years."

Elijah says, "That long?"

Enoch replies, "Yes, I hope that we will have some time to catch up."

Elijah responds, "We will have a little time. I arranged to have my next mission relatively close to here, so that I can postpone my departure a few hours. But I was not expecting such a crowd."

Enoch says, "Well, that's what you get for being a legend."

Elijah replies, "A legend, hardly. I am a poor man whom God, in His infinite mercy and compassion, chose to be gracious to and bless."

Enoch responds, "As humble as ever, I see. Come, almost everyone on the station is here to see you. Many have asked that you pray to God for His continued blessing and protection upon us."

Elijah walks to the center of the room and prays, "Lord God, Great Creator and Sustainer of all things, I thank you for placing a desire in these people's hearts to serve you and protect those who cannot protect themselves. I pray that you will look kindly upon them and continue to bless and protect each and every one of them. Guide them and strengthen them in Your ways. Give them Your knowledge and compassion, Your wisdom and Your love. Watch over them as a good father watches over his children. Thank you, Dear Lord."

Then and Elijah and all the people with him said, "Amen."

After Elijah finishes praying over the people, he and Enoch have lunch together. When Elijah leaves the room, the crowds begin to disband, and John comes over to David and Josh.

John smiles and says, "David, Josh, glad to see you."

Josh responds, "Good to see you, kid."

John replies, "I'm not exactly a kid anymore. I have graduated from Teutonic Squire to full-fledged Teutonic Knight."

David exclaims, "Already! You were assigned to be Elijah's squire only three years ago."

John, somewhat embarrassed, replies, "Actually, I graduated a year ago."

Josh jokingly says, "Well, I'm hurt. Here I've been a member of the Teutonic Knights five years longer than you and you have attained the same rank."

John jokingly replies, "Well, you can blame Elijah. It was his tutoring that did it."

David responds, "Speaking of you and Elijah, why are you still with him? If you've graduated, shouldn't he have a new squire and you have your own assignment?"

John replies, "When I graduated, Elijah and I asked Debra if Elijah could be allowed to continue instructing me, until the standard five-year period was up. She consented."

Josh says, "Wait a minute, after you graduated within only two years, you requested to remain with Elijah for another three? Aren't you the same idealistic John who was always saying that you couldn't wait to become a Teutonic knight? You wanted to graduate as soon as possible and fly off into uncharted sectors to preach to people who had never heard of Jehovah."

John replies, "Well, I still plan to do that, but Elijah has more faith than anyone I have ever met. There is still a lot more that I can learn from him."

There is a brief pause as that subject is finished, and then Josh says, "That is an impressive ship you have. It looks somewhat similar to Gunboat class, but much more advanced."

John replies, "It is Conscripter class—a new class of ships specially suited to the unanticipated and sometimes dangerous encounters of a Conscripter . It resembles a gunboat, because it is built on the same frame. However, it has an enhanced armor and weapon systems, along with some other new toys. Would you two like a tour?"

David responds, "Yes, I would love to see what new inventions our scientist have cooked up."

John says, "Well, come on."

The trio enter the ship. It does look impressive. There are a lot more switches, displays, and systems than a conventional gunboat. Josh notices that there doesn't seem to be any way to see out of the front of the ship. He asks John how the pilot can see where he is flying.

John responds, "The cockpit has a completely holographic display which provides the pilot and gunner with a three-dimensional image and readout of what is in front of the ship. This allows the entire front of the ship to be equipped with armor plating. Also, the holographic display is a lot more versatile than your standard cockpit window. It can be zoomed in on a specific spot so that you can better see what's happening. The display can also be rotated 360 degrees horizontally or vertically. This allows you to examine problems from different angles. In addition, we can switch views from the front of the ship to the back, sides, top, or the bottom of the ship with the push of a button, instead of having to look out windows on those sides."

David says, "It's incredible that our holographic technology has come this far. I remember when we needed a whole room just to view a simple hologram."

John says, "If you think that's incredible, follow me."

John leads David and Josh to the middle of the floor and waves his hand across a holographic projection of a symbol containing two crossed energy blades. A small compartment in the ceiling opens up and a hologram of a Teutonic Knight is projected. John pulls his energy blade and the hologram does the same. John moves his energy blade from side to side. The hologram matches his movements.

John says, "Within seven months, these will replace the Dueling Androids in most Teutonic practice arenas."

David asks, "How? It's a hologram—an image of light with no substance. How could you ever duel with it? Your blade and body would go right through it."

John replies, "Normally, yes, but our scientists have found a way to transmit a powerful gravitational field along the same light beams as those that make up the hologram. This gravitational field allows the hologram to block blows, strike, and even move solid objects."

Josh says, "That is impressive, but I don't know if it is such a good idea to make holograms that are capable of fighting. What if there is a short in the system, and the hologram tries to kill everyone around it?"

John responds, "There is a safety program written into the gravitational field's system that won't allow the field to become strong enough to really hurt anyone. If this program is damaged, the gravitational field automatically deactivates."

Josh says, "That's a good idea. What other toys does this ship have?"

John turns to his left, walks to the wall and waves his hand across a holographic projection of a hammer and anvil. The wall opens up and a machine five feet long, by three feet high, by two feet deep slides out. The top of the machine has two bins measuring two feet wide, by two long feet, by half a foot deep. In between the two bins are a scanning device, a holographic protector, and a verbal and touch interface panel.

David asks, "What's that?"

John replies, "This is an assembler station. The two bins contain microscopic construction robots, called assemblers. Given the proper materials, the assemblers can build any small device—from a laser shaver, to an audiovisual communicator, even a new energy blade. Of course, the more complex the item is to assemble, the longer it takes them to finish. Between the bins is a scanning device that makes a digital blueprint of virtually any small object's construction. Above the bins is a holographic projector that displays the blueprints and the chemical tables that are on file. At the bottom of the projector's midsection is a direct verbal interface which allows orders to be issued directly to the assemblers. Below the verbal interface is a holographic touch interface panel where alterations can be made to the stored blueprints and the chemical tables. The bottom section of the station houses a massive 5x2.5-foot chemical storage container which stores the chemicals that the assemblers require for construction. Finally, this entire station is hooked into the ship's computer core which allows the assemblers to access the blueprints of anything that the ship scans.

David says, "These things can construct any small object?"

John responds, "Well, no, they cannot build anything organic, and there have been one or two forms of metal that we haven't been able to break down into its base chemicals. Until we can, these metals cannot be duplicated. Since we cannot duplicate the metals, we cannot duplicate anything made out of them. Circumstances requiring a need for organic devices or something made out of these mystery metals are extremely rare and hardly worth mentioning.

Josh begins to say something, but is interrupted by a loud siren. The sound is accompanied by the station's lights changing from their normal color to a bright flashing red.

John asks, "What's that?"

David responds, "That's the station's defense alarm. It means that our early warning system has detected enemy forces on their way to the station."

Josh says, "Come on. We have to find out what's coming at us."

John goes to the cockpit and says, "I can tap into the station's monitors and use this ship's holographic display to find out what's coming." He activates the ship's holographic display and tells the ship to link up with the station's main monitors and display their image. The ships become visible, but the image is distorted.

David says, "I can barely make them out."

John says, "That's because we are using a double relay. I'll activate the ship's image enhancers. Give me a few seconds. The enemy ships become clearer and clearer, until they are perfectly represented.

As the image begins to become clearer, Josh says, "It looks like two carriers. And, oh, no! A battle wagon."

John asks, "Do you think the station's fighters can handle it?"

Josh responds, "Our station's fighters can probably handle their fighters and our station defenses can keep the carriers at bay. But if that battle wagon gets within range of the station, its main cannon will tear the station apart in less than ten minutes."

David says, "This doesn't make any sense. The Buccaneers were only able to get ahold of two battle wagons. Why would they risk one going after a fighter station? What could we have that would possibly be worth this to them?"

Josh says, "Does it really matter? There is no way that our fighters can take out the battle wagon, the two carriers, and their fighters."

John asks, "How long do we have?"

David answers, "Well, the battle wagon is slower than the carriers. I'd say we have about twenty minutes before the wagon is in firing range of the station."

John says, "And another six to eight minutes before its main cannon breaks through the station's deflector fields?"

Josh responds, "Yes. So?"

John replies, "The pirates got their ships from our mothball yards. So we should have the ship's blueprints on file." John moves his hands around several of the holographic interfaces. He brings up a section in the engine room.

John highlights one of the machines and says, "These are the ship's four quantum generators. If we can blow these up, that should take the entire engine room with it. The battle wagon won't even be able to activate emergency power. All it will have left for power is its batteries. The batteries will barely supply enough energy for artificial gravity and life support."

David responds, "But the battle wagon will shoot us down before we can get close enough for that plan to work."

Josh adds, "Another problem is that the engine room is surrounded by triple Tranakeium armor. We can't blast our way through that."

John replies, "Getting to the battle wagon won't be a problem. This ship has a new kind of stealth device that can't be detected even with quad spectrum scanners. Once we get to the battle wagon, we can use our ship's magnetic docking feet to attach to the side of it. Then we can use our boarding bay to get into the enemy ship. We get in, plant a few timed explosives, get out, and fly back here."

David says, "Okay, let's do it." Josh agrees. John opens the docking bay doors and takes the ship out.

While en route to the wagon, David asks John, "What is a boarding bay?"

John answers, "It is a small room with a large space lock positioned above three ripper beam projectors. The ripper beams work on the same principal as our energy beams, so they can cut through almost anything. They'll cut a hole through the ship's hull so that we can board the battle wagon."

Josh asks, "How long will it take to reach the battle wagon?"

John replies, "It'll take us about five minutes. We have that long to plan our attack."

David says, "A simple strategy will serve us best."

John responds, "Right. We go in invisible and make sure that we don't engage in any hostile behavior, until we reach the engine room. Once there, we plant the bombs and get out as quickly as we can."

Josh replies, "I can't turn invisible. I'm not trained for reconnaissance. I'm a pilot."

John says, "You are a Teutonic Knight. You serve the same God as David and I. We do not turn invisible. The Lord hides us from view. He can hide you just as well."

Josh responds, "I don't know if I have that kind of faith. I've never trained in it."

David replies, "Don't worry. We'll help you. While John's piloting the ship, I'll teach you as much as I can about infiltration faith building." However, Josh still looks unsure.

John finishes, "When the time comes, we'll all join hands as we pray. This will allow us to pool our faith. You'll be fine."

Josh says, "Okay." Then David begins to teach Josh his crash course.

When the Olive Branch reaches the battle wagon, David, Josh and John enter the boarding bay. There is a slight humming while the ripper beams cut into the battle wagon. It takes about thirty seconds for the ripper beams to finish cutting the opening which gives the three knights time to join hands and pray for God to hide them under the shadow of His wings. The ripper beams turn off and all the knights, including Josh, are hidden. John opens the space dock and tells his friends to watch their first step.

Josh asks, "Why?"

John answers, "Because the Olive Branch is docked onto the side of the enemy ship. When you step through the space dock, there will be a fourty-five difference in the relative gravity."

David goes first. He sits down on the rim of the space dock, and hangs his feet through the opening, until his feet are resting on the floor of the enemy ship. Then he pushes off of the rim and stands up.

David says, "Come on, it's no problem." Then Josh and John follow.

Josh sarcastically says, "Good, now that we're aboard the enemy battle wagon, all we've got to do is get to the engine room, plant the explosives and get back to our ship before they detonate."

David responds, "Yeah, sounds easy, doesn't it?"

John says, "According to the blueprints, the engine room should be right down this corridor."

Josh responds, "Well then, let's get a move on."

The three knights follow the corridor until they reach the engine room. Upon entering the room, they see several pirate engineers. The engineers are working on some strange looking dueling androids (D.A.).

John, not wanting to be overheard, whispers, "What are they doing?"

Josh whispers back, "I don't know, but I think it might be important that we find out. How many people do you need to plant the explosives?"

John quietly responds, "If I had to, I could do it myself."

Josh whispers, "Good, I'll probably be done in time to help you anyway, but I've got a feeling that there's something important about these D.A.s, and I'd like to get a closer look at them." Then Josh heads toward the engineers and their D.A.s.

David whispers, "I'm going to use that computer terminal to activate a gas leak alarm which should get everyone out of here. Once we begin planting explosives, we will become visible. It would be best if no one was around to see us. Besides, when the explosives detonate, this room's going to go kaboom. It would be best to try to limit the casualties."

John says, "Okay, I'll wait for the alarm. Then I'll begin planting the explosives. But try to hurry. We only have about ten more minutes before the station is within this battle wagon's weapon range. And we need five of those ten to get back to our ship."

David activates the gas leak alarm. The pirate engineers dash out of the room. As the last engineer leaves, he attempts to contain the gas leak by hitting a button on the wall outside the engine room. The engine room's blast doors begin to close. When Josh sees the blast doors closing, he rushes toward the button on the other side, but he is too late. The blast doors seal John, Josh and David inside the engine room.

John says, "That's okay. Josh and David, while the two of you use your energy blades to cut through these blast doors, I'll plant the explosives."

David says, "Okay." But when he and Josh draw their energy blades and become visible, the dueling androids activate.

David turns to John and says, "You go plant the explosives. Josh and I will handle those androids."

John asks, "Are you sure?"

David replies, "A few dueling androids, yes, I'm sure."

John says, "Okay." John is still hidden and able to slip by the advancing dueling androids. He heads for the back of the engine room where the quantum generators are located.

As David and Josh charge the advancing D.A.s, Josh says, "I guess I'm going to get an even closer look at these androids than I intended."

Both knights let out a laugh as they reach their enemies.

David slashes at one of the D.A.'s chest plates, but the D.A. uses its energy blade to deflect the blow. Another D.A. gets behind David, raises its energy blade up above David's head, and thrusts downward. David leaps out of the way. As he does, still another D.A. grabs him in mid-air and begins to squeeze the life out of him. David is able to move his energy blade just enough to cut off one of the D.A.'s arms. Now free, David falls to the ground and rolls away from the amputated android, tripping another D.A. that's just about to overpower Josh.

David stands up as Josh says, "Thanks."

The tripped D.A. stands back up. David and Josh notice that more of the androids are coming toward them. David notices that the D.A. whose arm was cut off, is stooping down to grab his severed arm and watches as the D.A. brings the arm's two severed edges together. Several small metallic bands come out of the D.A.'s severed parts and reattach themselves. Josh throws his laser disk straight through one of the D.A.'s chest plates. The D.A. stammers a little, but David and Josh see the same kind of metallic bands go across the hole and repair it.

David asks Josh, "What did those engineers do to these D.A.s?"

Josh responds, "My guess is that the Buccaneers wanted a ground unit capable of fighting off Teutonic Knights. So they tuned up some of their ship's dueling androids. They must have increased their strength, attached blast-poof armor, and apparently installed some kind of autorepair system."

Just then, John catapults over the oncoming "Enhanced Dueling Androids." As he passes over them, he turns his blade and manages to decapitate three of the E.D.A.s.

John lands and says, "I've finished with the explosives and thought you could use some help."

Then David, Josh and John see the three decapitated E.D.A.s bend down and feel around until they find their heads. Once they find their heads, the three E.D.A.s reattach their heads in the same way that the other E.D.A. reattached his arm.

As the three knights begin to back away, David says, "Those things are unstoppable!"

The E.D.A.s start advancing on the three knights as John replies, "I've got an idea. Hand me your energy blades."

Josh responds, "Are you kidding? Without our energy blades to at least slow them down, those bots will cut through us in no time."

John answers, "You can hold them off for a little while with your laser disks. I think that there's an adjustment that can be made to the blades that should increase their effectiveness."

David and Josh hand John their blades and attempt to slow the E.D.A.s' advance. David, being the one with more ground combat experience, tells Josh to cover him as he takes the lead.

One of the E.D.A.s strikes at David. David tightens his grip on his laser disk and with one fluid motion deflects the blow, spins around the outside of the E.D.A.'s arm, and cuts through the E.D.A.'s neck. David finds himself between two E.D.A.s. Both raise their blades and slice down at David's throat. David doesn't have enough time to block both blows, so dropping onto his back, he dodges the attack and causes the two E.D.A.s to cut through each other's torsos. The E.D.A.s upper bodies drop to the floor, followed shortly by their lower bodies. As David tries to get back onto his feet, another E.D.A. grabs him with both hands and holds him in place, while a second E.D.A prepares to run David through. Josh lets his laser disk fly. The disk cuts through the center of the two E.D.A.s' heads. As the upper half of the heads fall, David kicks the halves away from the wholes. The E.D.A. holding David releases his grip, allowing David to drop and land on his two feet.

The two E.D.A.s forget about David as they scamper about searching for the other half of their heads. David allows a grin to spread across his face as he momentarily watches the comical scene. David's respite is cut short as the first three E.D.A.s, having repaired their damaged bodies regroup and once again go after the two knights.

David and Josh hear John say, "Got it!" John tosses them their blades, and continues, "Try them now."

The three Teutonic Knights charge the E.D.A.s. John leaps over one's head and tries to cut downward across its neck, but he E.D.A. blocks the blow with its energy blade. David sees an opening and cuts off the E.D.A.'s arm. The arm and blade fall to the floor. The E.D.A. reaches down, reclaiming its arm, but as it tries to bring the two cut edges together, the E.D.A. discovers that they are being pushed apart by an invisible force. The E.D.A. applies more pressure to the detached arm. The other androids notice their brother's trouble and stop their advance. The three knights also observe this strange contest. The first E.D.A. continues to struggle against its invisible force. It finally manages to get the edges close enough for the metallic bands to bridge the gap between the E.D.A.'s arm and body. But as soon as the E.D.A. moves its hand away from the injured arm, in its attempt to resume the battle, the bands snap and the injured arm flies across the room imbedding itself in a computer console.

After a couple of seconds, the severed arm and the injured E.D.A. explode.

Josh gives an approving whistle and asks John, "Just what did you do to our blades?"

John answers, "I retuned the energy emitters to project a blade of electric magnetic energy instead of a laser. The blade cut through the E.D.A.'s arm and gave both the wound and the arm a positive electromagnetic charge. Since like charges repel, I figured that the E.D.A. wouldn't be able to reattach its severed parts, but I don't know why the E.D.A. exploded."

David responds, "These androids must have a failsafe that automatically destroys them, if they are unable to repair themselves within a certain time frame."

Josh replies, "Makes sense, I doubt the Buccaneers would want to give us a chance to study their modifications."

John says, "Well, that should make it even easier to defeat these E.D.A.s, but we had better stand back after we injure them. We don't want to be too close when they self-destruct."

David, Josh, and John make quick work of the rest of the E.D.A.s. Then they cut their way through the blast doors and head back to the Olive Branch. Once aboard the Olive Branch, John uses his remote detonator to activate the timer on the explosives.

Josh asks, "How long do we have?"

John Replies, "I set the timer for three minutes. That gives us plenty of time to get to a safe distance."

The Olive Branch separates from the enemy battle wagon. The battle wagon's auto pressure doors close, sealing off the small section of corridor with the hole in it from the rest of the ship. Then the Olive Branch heads back toward Ace Squadron station.

As the Olive Branch heads toward Ace Squadron Station, John sees that one of the Teutonic fighters is severely outmatched. John says, "We're going into the fight. It looks like one of your friends could use some help."

David looks at the lone fighter and exclaims, "That's Esther's fighter!"

Josh says, "What? We've got to help her."

John says, "We're going as fast as we can. She'll have to hold out for a few more minutes."

Josh exclaims, "Well, open communications! If she heads toward us, it will cut down the time."

David responds, "I've already tried. Her ship's communications are out. The good news is that I've scanned the enemy fighters and it looks like everyone who had missiles has already launched them. All that we should have to worry about is their laser cannons."

John says, "We are almost within weapons range. Josh, you man the turret. David, I'm turning over flight and main weapons control to you. Tell me when you're ready."

David sits in the pilot's seat, grabs the fighter joysticks, and says, "Ready."

John transfers control. David asks, "What are you going to do?"

John replies, "I'm going to use this ship's Mosquito Drones."

The Olive Branch approaches the fray, and David asks, "What is a Mosquito Drone?"

John answers, "A Mosquito Drone is a small unmanned ship equipped with a class one laser array, a scanning device and a transmitter-receiver dish. I can launch all five of this ship's Mosquitoes and control them from the main console."

The Olive Branch gets within optimum scanning range of most of the enemy fighters, and John says, "Heads up. Here they come."

Eight enemy fighters break off from attacking Esther's fighter and launch a frontal attack on the Olive Branch. David takes out three of them. Josh gets one and wings another. The remaining fighters take some pot shots as they pass. Josh rotates his turret while firing at the enemy fighters. He gets one more. The other two split up and make a run on both sides of the Olive Branch. John uses his Mosquitoes to blow one fighter away as it begins its pass. Then John swings his Mosquitoes around the Olive Branch's stern and goes after the other fighter. The Mosquitoes, being faster than a fighter, catch up to the last enemy fighter and take it out.

Josh says, "All right! Not so tough when you don't have overwhelming odds."

Just then David says, "Oh, no! One of the enemy fighters has pierced the armor around Esther's fighter's quantum drive. One more hit in that area and…"

Esther's fighter blows up before David can finish his statement. Josh screams, "NO! David, please tell me she ejected her cockpit in time."

David says, "Her cockpit separated right before the fighter exploded, but the explosion severely damaged the cockpit and all its systems, including life support. If we don't get to her within the next few minutes, she'll run out of air—if she's not dead already."

Then David, Josh and John notice ten more enemy fighters converging on them. Josh says, "Come on, you filthy dogs. I'll make you all pay for what you've done to Esther."

Josh rotates his turret and blasts away at one of the enemy fighters, until it blows up into a fiery ball. Then Josh rotates his turret and begins on the next enemy fighter. He continues to repeat the cycle. David takes out two of the enemy fighters that are charging from the front. John flies his Mosquitoes toward an enemy fighter and uses the Mosquitoes' laser arrays to set up an energy web right in front of the enemy fighter. The enemy pilot cannot stop in time. As he flies through the energy web, his weapon's systems and thrusters are literally cut off. Then John uses the same procedure on the next fighter. Finally, all ten enemy fighters have been taken out, but the knights don't have any time to rest. Another wave of pirate fighters charge their ship.

David says, "We can't keep this up! My cannons are running out of power."

John replies, "Okay. I will program the computer for a quick quantum jump. That'll recharge the systems."

Josh responds, "You can't. Even a quick jump will move us too far from Esther. We've got to keep those fighters away from her cockpit. From now on, we hold our fire until we have a clean shot. One shot, one hit, everyone got that?"

David and John reply, "Got it."

The enemy fighters draw near. This time David, Josh and John hold their fire until they are sure that they won't miss.

The enemy fighters come in with cannons blazing. Because the Olive Branch doesn't return fire, the enemy pilots assume that the last wave disabled the Olive Branch's weapons control. The enemy fighter pilots begin to drop their guard. Their approach is direct, with no evasive maneuvers. In order to wear down the Olive Branch's deflector fields faster, the enemy pilots transfer power from their ship's deflectors to their weapons systems.

John says, "What's wrong with these pilots? They're coming straight at us, and according to my scanners, their deflectors barely have enough power to protect them from a dust cloud."

David reasons that the enemy pilots think the Olive Branch's weapons are out. He tells Josh and John, "Hold your fire until they are within optimum weapons range. Then set your weapons to wide dispersal and fire at the center of their formation."

Josh and John do as David suggests. When they finally do fire, they take out all but one of the fighters in the enemy formation. The last fighter vanishes.

David says, "That fighter must have a stealth device."

John responds, "Give me a few seconds. This ship has a class seven scanning system. I should be able to find him."

John hits a few holographic keys, and then says, "I've got him. Oh, no, he still has his a missile and is about to fire!"

The enemy pilot says, "You've caused enough trouble." The enemy pilot fires.

Right before the missile impacts, a Teutonic pilot slams the side of her fighter into the side of the missile, knocking it off course. Then it executes a tight turn and blows the enemy fighter away. In order to thank the pilot, John opens communications.

John says, "Thank you, whoever you are. You've sure got talent."

Esther responds, "Thanks. Glad I could help."

David says, "Esther?"

Esther replies, "Of course. Surprised to see me?"

Josh responds, "Yes! Your fighter was destroyed, and we've been trying to keep these pirates away from the cockpit."

Esther replies, "I couldn't get to my regular fighter. When we discovered that the station was under attack by two carriers and a battle wagon, the fighter pilots had to mobilize quickly. Everyone rushed to whichever fighter was closest and took off."

Josh sees that all the remaining enemy fighters are headed at them. Josh says, "Oh, come on, you've got to be kidding. There's no way that we're going to survive this." The enemy fighters fly closer.

David says, "All right, everyone get ready."

John says, "Here they come." But to everyone's surprise, the enemy fighters fly right by.

Esther says, "What?"

John scans the area and replies, "The explosives have detonated, the battle wagon is disabled and the Buccaneers are retreating."

The Olive Branch swings over and picks up the cockpit of Esther's usual fighter. The pilot is unconscious, but alive.

Josh says, "Come on, everyone, let's head back to the station." The Olive Branch and the fighter Esther's piloting head back to Ace Squadron station.

On the way, David says, "By the way, when I was going through the Buccaneer's computer system, I found out what it is that they wanted bad enough to risk a battle wagon."

John asks, "What?"

David replies, "They were trying to get hold of Crinice's inverted gateway. The Buccaneers have been getting weaker and weaker since the increase in Teutonic pilots and the treaty with the Privateers. They must have decided that they would be defeated unless they could get hold of one of our inverted gateways."

Esther says, "Yeah, with an inverted gateway they could loot and steal from ships anywhere. Just use the inverted gateway to get aboard, kill or imprison the crew, take control of the ship and fly it back to a Buccaneer base."

Josh asks, "But the Buccaneers discovered long ago that whenever they take a planet that has one of our inverted gateways, the Teutonics on that planet activate the inverted gateway's self-destruct program. The gateway is useless long before the Buccaneers can get to it."

Josh adds, "Yeah, so why would the Buccaneers think that Crinice would be any different?"

David answers, "Because with all the problems that Crinice has had with its inverted gateway lately, it has been completely deactivated while our engineers make repairs. The deactivation includes all subsystems—even the self-destruct. The Buccaneers must have intercepted one of the messages that we sent to Brotherhood informing them of the condition of Crinice's inverted gateway."

Esther responds, "I see. So they destroy Ace Squadron station, take control of the planet it orbits, either force our engineers into repairing the inverted gateway or use their engineers, and finally put the inverted gateway aboard the battle wagon and head off."

David replies, "That also explains those enhanced dueling androids they were working on. The Buccaneers' security force would never stand a chance against the Teutonic Knights on the planet's surface, but those E.D.A.s are a different story. Looks like your guess was right on the mark, Josh." Josh smiles.

John says, "Then it's a good thing that we, with God's help, were able to stop them."

Josh responds, "Yeah, I'd hate to imagine what the Buccaneers would do with an inverted gateway." The others within the Olive Branch agree, and John leads them in a prayer of thanks.

As the knights head back to Ace Squadron station, David thinks about everything that has happened since the Teutonics began the evacuation from their beloved home planet—Earth. David thinks about the different planets that he has been to. He remembers the adventures he has had and the people he has met. As David thinks about Sara, his thoughts linger on their love for each other. He thinks about Sara's faithful spirit, her beautiful face, and that sweet voice of hers that holds the promise of softness. David longs to be near her again. Then he remembers the promise he has given to her father, the King, to wait two years until he sees her again. He is exceedingly sad. Teutonic Knights never go back on their word, so it will be a long time before he sees Sarah again. He remembers the friends he has made—friends like Gruchase, Esther, Zipporah and Doulphla. Remembering them helps cheer him up. Finally, David thinks about the future. He wonders what excitement is waiting for him when he travels past the borders of known Teutonic space—finding lost colonies, spreading God's word and welcoming those who are willing to join the Teutonic Union. David decides that being a Conscripter might just be the best assignment he has ever had.

Printed in Great Britain
by Amazon